1ᵃ US
5 —
m

Darling Corey's Dead

Martha G. Webb

·*Darling Corey's Dead*·

Walker and Company ❋ *New York*

First published in the United States of America
in 1984 by the Walker Publishing Company, Inc.

Published simultaneously in Canada by John Wiley & Sons
Canada, Limited, Rexdale, Ontario.

Library of Congress Cataloging in Publication Data

Webb, Martha G.
      Darling Corey's dead.

      I. Title.
PS3573.E196D3   1984   813'.54   83-21735
ISBN 0-8027-5582-8

Library of Congress Catalog Card Number: 83-21735

Printed in the United States of America

10 9 8 7 6 5 4 3 2 1

"Wake up, wake up, Darling Corey,
What makes you sleep so sound?"

—American folk song

To the general public, the Postal Inspection Service is probably the least known law enforcement agency in the country. In the opinion of the author, it is also the best law enforcement agency in the country.

·*Prologue*·

In her mind, she saw that June as a pastiche glued together with blood.

Darling Corey's dead—no loss, but a change, a change from what had been standard and accepted as long as Cheryl had been policing (and Allen could have been dead, too—only he wasn't—that time).

The month began with death, on a clear blue afternoon, and although the lab report made it plain whose pistol had made that impossible shot into a second-story window she still couldn't quite believe it; because it happened so slowly and so fast at the same time that she didn't have a chance to realize it then, and afterwards too much else was happening for her to spare a thought for that.

The month ended with death, also quite sudden. She remembered him still with one knee under him, sprawled in the blood on the newlv cut green grass, one hand reaching into the roses . . .

For the pistol . . .

. . . That they had looked for all of June, the .32 Omega with ten lands and grooves and a right-hand twist . . .

That had been hidden in a tin box under the rose trellis in that quite innocent yard.

That one she could believe. That one she could remember. It shouldn't have been necessary; she'd said, "Stop or I'll shoot," but he just couldn't quite believe she really would.

But oddly enough, her clearest single memory of that entire month was of Holly crying in the street and climbing the tailgate of Waymon's pickup truck while sirens sang in the distance.

·One·

*T*he first shot rang out seconds after they had slammed the car door, startling them both with its utter unexpectedness and shattering the windshield between them. Cheryl, on the street side of the blue Ford, dropped down behind it onto the dirt shoulder, almost even with the front of the back door. She reached for the short-barrelled .38 in the shoulder holster under her shirt jacket as Allen Conyers, with one shocked glance at the house, rolled across the hood of the car to join her. He had his service revolver out by the time he landed beside her.

"Where'd it come from?" Allen shouted, rather too close to Cheryl's ear for comfortable shouting.

"I don't know," Cheryl answered, moving away from him. "Up there somewhere."

"Up there somewhere" covered a lot of territory. The old three-story Victorian mansion had been converted into apartments thirty years before, and they must have been slum apartments for over twenty of those years, but all the same, there were twenty-four windows overlooking the bare dirt yard.

There hadn't been another shot yet to tell them where the sniper was.

"What the *hell?*" Allen said, more quietly. "All I wanted to do was *talk* to her, for crying out loud."

"That's not going to be her doing the shooting," Cheryl answered.

"No?" Allen asked dubiously. "You already told me she'd gotten away with killing two people."

"But they were both on account of drug rip-offs," Cheryl answered. "She doesn't shoot at cops. At least, she hasn't before. I don't have any extra ammo," she added. "Do you?"

"Yeah, but it's in the glove box, and I don't know if I can get to it." He glanced again, apprehensively, at the house.

"I'm shorter than you. I can get it if you'll give me the car key."

"If I haven't dropped it—" He didn't argue about safety; he just handed over the key. The instant she reached for it a second shot rang out, ricocheting off the hood of the car and lodging in a live oak tree in the yard. They both fired back, but too late; the gunman had stepped back again into the darkened room behind the window.

But at least they knew, now, which window.

Cheryl scrabbled in the dirt for the car key and said, "Cover me." She opened the door slightly as Allen, revolver in hand, cautiously peered over the hood. She could reach both the glove box and the walkie-talkie, on the floor partway under the seat, without actually getting in the car, but she still had to stand a little higher than she wanted to, because the pouch of bullets had slid to the back of the glove box. As she reached for it, two shots cracked at the same time, and something stung the top of her left shoulder.

It was, quite literally, only a bad scratch, but the gunpowder made the cut burn like a hot iron, and Cheryl said a very bad word.

"*What* did you say?" Allen demanded.

"I said expletive deleted," Cheryl answered, and added, "damn it!" Her shoulder went on burning.

"Are you okay?"

"Yeah, I'm just mad." She finally juggled the radio into a usable position. "Officers need help at 1804 South Coolidge. We are pinned down by sniper fire." The radio was silent. "Car 17 to headquarters?" The radio stayed silent, but the sniper didn't; another shot knocked out the driver's side window.

Cheryl fired back twice to Allen's once, and Allen said, "You better save your ammunition. I wonder if I can circle around and get to the door of the house?"

Without waiting for Cheryl to answer, he took three running steps away from the car. He dashed back behind the car as four shots hit the ground, tracking toward him, and said breathlessly, "That didn't work."

It was useless for Cheryl to try to raise the detective bureau on the radio, because Kathy always turned the monitor off when she was working on the FBI report. "Look," Cheryl said, "if we crawl under the car, and he doesn't know how to use the ricochet effect right, we can get a lot better shot at him."

"And if we crawl under the car, and he does know how to use the ricochet effect right, we can both get dead," Allen pointed out. Another bullet sang off the hood, and they both fired back ineffectually again.

Sitting with her back to the front wheel, Cheryl began to reload. "Have you got any better ideas?" she demanded. "Because he's got at least two guns up there—a pistol and a rifle."

"Make that three," Allen replied, as shotgun pellets peppered the ground directly behind them, coming from over the roof of the car in an arched trajectory. Allen fired twice more and then snapped on an empty.

"You didn't count," Cheryl chided, and slid the box of ammo toward him. She kneeled tall to cover him while he reloaded. "What've you got, a five-shot carried on an empty?"

"Chief Special. Yeah, it's a five-shot." He scrambled to his feet again, crouching behind the fender with the revolver gripped in both hands and aimed at the window.

"How many damn people have we got up there?" Cheryl demanded.

"One," Allen said definitely. "At least three weapons, but he's firing them one at a time." He ducked and fired simultaneously as a rifle shot passed perilously near his head, and of course, his shot went wild. "Okay, you're right, we go under the car, because he's about got our range. Let me go between the rear wheels, and you go between the front wheels."

That put them crossing one in front of the other, and it put Allen, considering the position of the car, in a slightly more exposed spot. Cheryl, at the moment, didn't feel disposed to argue the matter. One of them had to get there.

They crawled into position, and she tried again to key the radio. "It's not even getting out now," she said.

"Are you sure it was before?" Allen asked.

"Yeah, it's just the body of the car blocking it."

"God, though, you'd think *somebody* would call the police."

"*Here?*" Cheryl said bitterly. "Hah!"

A rifle bullet smacked the concrete walk in front of the car, ricocheted underneath, and noisily blew out a rear tire. Allen grunted and half rolled over. "Are you okay?" Cheryl asked sharply as the hot rubbery tire fumes floated toward her.

"I think so," Allen said.

But his voice sounded rather strained. He did not, she thought, sound okay.

"Are you sure that's not Darling Corey up there?" Allen asked, still sounding somewhat breathless.

"Yeah," Cheryl said. "I told you it wasn't. It's not her speed. If she was going to shoot us, she'd walk right up to us, looking cute, and then fire point-blank."

"If that's not her, then who is it?" Allen demanded, and added, "What's a bitch like that still doing on the street anyway?"

"Don't ask me," Cheryl replied to the second question rather than the obviously unanswerable first. "Allen, you idiot," she added suddenly, "you're left-handed and your left arm is blocked, and I'm right-handed and my right arm is blocked. We ought to be in exactly opposite positions to what we are." She began to crawl forward, out from under the car, adding, "I guess if you're going to murder somebody, it helps to be little and cute. You ought to see Darling Corey charm an all-male jury."

"Damn you, Cheryl," Allen said, "get your ass back under here." He began to move forward also.

"Don't try to baby me," Cheryl told him.

"Baby you hell," Allen retorted. "I'm trying to stay alive, and I wish you'd do the same. Good God, he's hit this sidewalk twice." By now they were both almost to the sidewalk, and Cheryl could see the grey splatter of lead where the last slug had hit the ground . . . and she could see blood dripping slowly to the ground just under Allen's left armpit, easily visible because he was lying on his stomach, propped up on his elbows.

Allen swore again, furiously, and Cheryl said, "Allen?" Her voice sounded sharp in her own ears; incongruously, she suddenly became aware of a pounding headache.

"It's a goddamn fire ant," he said, and slapped at his gun hand with his right hand. "Ouch, damn, goddamn, I've got a bed of fire ants over here." He rapidly moved about a foot closer to Cheryl.

They still had not returned that last shot. In a third-floor window a man with a shotgun in his hand leaned incautiously a little too far forward, trying to see where they'd gone. Very deliberately, Cheryl fired at his chest, hearing Allen fire a split second later. They could see both bullets hit as if on a silhouette target, and the man, still holding the shotgun, toppled slowly out the window.

Allen scrambled to his feet, peeled off his jacket, and began to dust ants off his left arm, totally oblivious of the blood that was trickling down his side. "You're going to be sick from those bites," Cheryl told him.

"No shit, Sherlock," Allen replied angrily, and then, rather sheepishly, he said, " 'Scuse me. It's not your fault. It just hurts like hell. I never got bitten by a fire ant before and I hope I never do again."

Cheryl laughed aloud, and Allen demanded, "What's so funny?"

"You've been shot," Cheryl pointed out, "and you haven't even said 'ouch' about that yet, and you're standing there throwing a fit about ant bites?"

"Have you ever been bitten by a fire ant?"

"Yes," Cheryl said, "and I don't blame you a bit for swearing. I'd help you remove them, but one of us needs to keep an eye on King Kong over there, just in case he's playing possum."

"No sense both of us getting bit. I think I've got them all off now, anyway. Let's go check on him."

Cautiously, pistols still out, they approached the body.

It was definitely a body. The condition of the head, which had hit a guy wire on the way down, left no doubt about that.

"Car 17?" said the radio apologetically. "Were you trying to raise the station a while ago? I was ten-six on the phone."

You're always ten-six when I need you, Cheryl thought viciously and quite untruthfully. "I wanted," she said precisely, "to tell you that the postal inspector and I were under fire and needed help. But *now* I want to tell you that the sniper needs the coroner, and Allen and I want EMS. It is not," she added, "ten-eighteen. None of us are going anywhere just now."

Allen's face had turned a little pale, but he was laughing. "And you call Darling Corey a bitch! Come here, vixen, you look like you want to cry, and it's much too late to cry now."

Ridiculously, she did want to cry. "I'm just so darn mad," she explained. "Where were you hit? I can't tell. You're bleeding all over your shirt."

"Ah, it just grazed the outside of a rib high on the left side. I don't think I even got the whole slug; I think it broke when it hit the tire. I'm not hurt any more than you, but it kind of knocked the breath out of me for a second. Damn it, though, it was a new suit."

"So was mine," Cheryl said. "At least, kind of new. I wonder if his was?"

"Doesn't look like it, does it? He is some kind of grungy."

By now the air was full of sirens, so they both leaned on the trunk of the car and waited for the ambulance to arrive.

Cheryl decided she didn't want to cry after all, but she wished the headache would let up.

A detective car jerked to a halt behind them, and Sergeant Hall erupted out of it, his tie as usual slightly on one side and his coat left behind somewhere. "Cheryl Burroughs, what the hell do you think you're doing?"

"Waiting for EMS," Cheryl replied accurately, knowing she was not responding at all to the real question.

"Now don't get cute at me."

"I brought her with me," Allen said, "because I wanted to talk with Darling Corey Wilson about some forged checks, and with what I've heard about Darling Corey I thought I might better bring a female officer with me."

That wasn't quite true. He'd wanted any detective he could get to go along with him as a backup, but he hadn't thought of Cheryl until, thoroughly bored with the thefts and vandalisms she'd been working for the last three weeks, she asked him to take her along.

"I couldn't ask you about it," he went on, "because you were in that meeting, and so I finally just told her to come on and I'd get straight with you later. And then when we got out of the car that bastard, whoever he was, started shooting at us."

Sergeant Hall walked over and looked at the body, running his hands through his greying blond hair as he stood. He came back. "He's not local, whoever he is. I never saw him before. But he looks familiar all the same."

A green car stopped and two men in business suits got out. One of them asked cheerfully, "Playing like you're a target, huh, Allen? Is it a fun game?"

"What the hell are you doing here?" the sergeant demanded, not too pleased to see the FBI at the scene of a killing.

"Been to Texarkana and headed for Tyler, and we'd about decided to stop in and visit you when your radio got all excited. What've you got going on?"

"You two are supposed to investigate assaults on federal officers,"

Allen pointed out from his perch on the trunk of his car. "So investigate already."

"But that's just why we came," one of the agents said. "We heard you needed an ambulance. But now here you are up walking around, and it doesn't even look like there's much investigating to do since the suspect is, uh, taken care of. What've you got, a skinned rib?"

His expression and tone of voice were somewhat more serious than his words, and he added, "Are you okay, Allen?" A skinned rib bleeds even more than a body shot, and by now Allen was looking distinctly gory; Cheryl, hit high on the left arm, was scarcely bleeding at all.

"Yeah, sure, I'm fine," Allen answered, and added, "Watch out for the ant hill."

The warning came a little late, and the younger FBI agent used some language J. Edgar wouldn't have approved of. The older agent quipped, "Sure he's okay. That's because he brought Cheryl along for protection." He walked over to look at the body. Then, with a barely audible exclamation, he knelt over it, abruptly forgetting the crease in his grey trousers. "And none of you know who this is? Haven't any of you ever heard of Jimmie Pitts?" he demanded, looking closely at one of the corpse's grimy hands.

Quite suddenly, all eyes were on the body. Allen vaulted off the trunk of the car and headed toward it, Cheryl right behind him.

"Are you sure, Darren?" Sergeant Hall asked doubtfully.

"I'm sure," the agent said. "I arrested him myself once about four years back, for an interstate con job. While I was transporting him he gave me a lengthy dissertation on how to avoid leaving fingerprints. I learned a lot from it." He pointed down. "Even if you forget the face, look at that scar on the wrist. He got it from a kerosene stove when he was a kid. You wouldn't forget that."

"No, I guess not," Allen agreed softly, looking at the reverse image of three letters from the brand name of the stove.

Hall rounded on him. "Go sit down, damn it, and quit bleeding on the damn evidence. You're damn well supposed to be waiting for an ambulance."

"Three damns in one breath," Allen said. Collecting Cheryl on the way, he went back and sat on the curb.

Jimmie Pitts was that rare creature, a con man turned violent. He'd been a good con man, professionally speaking. He'd worked some flim-flams but had been best known for kite flying and paperhanging, lines of work which have nothing whatever to do with March breezes or bathroom walls but are concerned rather with the fraudulent use of checks.

But one day not quite three years before, a deputy sheriff in a little Louisiana jail had roughed Jimmie up a bit more than Jimmie considered acceptable and then, contemptuous of the usually meek con man, had turned his back. The deputy sheriff had bled to death before an ambulance could reach him, and since then, an Arkansas trooper and a Dallas city policeman had died from bullets indisputably fired from the .357 Jimmie took from the deputy.

Two months ago, Jimmie Pitts had made the Ten Most Wanted list. And now he was dead, in the bare red clay yard of a small town in northeast Texas, from bullets fired from the service revolvers of a five-foot-tall policewoman and a forty-two-year-old postal inspector.

"Well, well, well," said Sergeant Hall bemusedly, and looked around. Cheryl was now perched on the tailgate of an ambulance with an emergency medical technician putting a temporary bandage on her arm. Allen, sitting on the front bumper of his own car, was taking his shirt off and looked a little annoyed. Hall went over and sat beside him on the bumper, ignoring the fact that he was getting in the way of the EMT. "Cheryl give you any trouble?" he asked.

Cheryl, supposedly out of earshot, listened for the answer. "Did you expect her to?" Allen asked. "I assume you know her."

Hall looked around at the corpse. "Right now," he said, "I'm not at all sure I do."

"Then what do you need me to tell you?" Allen asked. "Look, I need somebody local to ride with me the rest of this week, because I'm getting a lot of nicknames from snitches and I need somebody who can maybe identify some of them. Can you lend me Cheryl?"

"You said something about that on Tuesday," Hall reminded him, "and I was going to loan you Lloyd."

"Shi-yut," Allen said, making the word two syllables, and then dropped his voice so low that Cheryl had to strain to hear. "Just to remind you of something you seem to have forgotten, you loaned me Lloyd the second week I was in town, and he promptly ran out on me when Billy Joe Pinson started that ruckus."

"Yeah, well, but—"

"There's no 'yeah, well, but' to it. I know he says he was trying to get some help, but damn it, whatever reason he gave, he did run, and he left Pinson holding my gun on me, and it was nothing in the world but pure luck that I talked Pinson into giving up. And Pinson wouldn't have got the gun to start with if Lloyd had been backing me up like he should have been. If you think I've forgiven or forgotten that, you better think again. If you won't let me borrow Cheryl, then I'll take someone else or go alone, but I don't get in a car with Lloyd Methvin again. Look, I'm beginning to feel like this is a dangerous town."

"You can use Cheryl and welcome," Hall said, "but she's going nowhere else today. She's off duty the rest of the day no matter what the doctor says, and if you've got good sense you are too. And this was *not* a dangerous town until you came in and got it all stirred up."

Allen grinned. "Maybe you're right at that. As far as taking off, we're neither one of us really hurt, but I know I'm shook up and I figure Cheryl is too. Look, if your boys can locate Darling Corey, put a hold on her for me, would you? And tell the wrecker to take my car somewhere that they can put some new glass in it."

"Will do," Hall said.

"Hey, if you dudes would can the chatter," an EMT said, "we need to get these two transported."

In the hospital, an orderly put them both in the same room, drew a chaste curtain between them, and left, shutting the door. Allen got up and opened the curtain and then got back up on the high table. "Now I suppose we wait two hours," he said, scratching at one of the ant bites.

"If we wait past an hour, I'm leaving," Cheryl said. "Except I can't really do that, can I?"

"Nope. 'Fraid not."

"Thank you for taking me with you," she said, in a polite mockery of little girl manners.

Allen laughed again. He was, Cheryl decided, a very laughy sort of person. "You're quite welcome," he answered, with a formal politeness matching hers. "But," he added, "next time you ride with me, I hope to hell it's not that exciting a ride."

As Cheryl and Allen had been leaving the police station at two o'clock that muggy June afternoon, Darling Corey had paused, with one gold hoop earring in her hand, to glance over at the rumpled bed. Jimmie was snoring steadily, oblivious of the June heat. Which was unusual. In the three days she had known Jimmie he'd refused to sleep at all in the daytime, and he hadn't really slept much at night, either. Crashing now, Darling Corey guessed.

She didn't know that she thought much of Jimmie Pitts. But the Man had said to look after him, and so she was looking after him. As far as she was concerned, Jimmie came out of nowhere and would undoubtedly go back to nowhere later, when his business with the Man that had brought him to Lakeport was finished. In the meantime, she didn't much care what he did.

One good thing about Jimmie, he had plenty of bread and he didn't much care how fast it went as long as he was the one deciding how to spend it. But he never wanted to *go* anywhere, he just stayed holed up here all the time, and Darling Corey liked to go places. That dance at the Amvet tonight, now. Jimmie probably wouldn't want to go, and she couldn't even go by herself, not now, when the Man had said she had to look after Jimmie.

The second earring in place, she turned her attention to a third coat of lemon-yellow gloss on her long fingernails. Then, putting the bottle down, she looked distastefully at the dressing table, with its three drawers down each side of the kneehole and the round ornately framed mirror that so badly needed resilvering. God, how she hated this place!

Well, hate it or not, she was stuck here for a while longer. But with just a little more bread she could at least get some new furniture, maybe that Mediterranean suite with the red velvet inlays she'd seen last week at Luke's Furniture Discount. Only a hundred and sixty-nine dollars for the dressing table, and Jimmie would never miss it. She looked wistfully at the roll he carried.

Even now, with Jimmie asleep after the two joints she'd given him, she didn't quite dare risk it. He'd looked at her that first day with those cold green eyes set in that hawk-shaped brown face, and said, "Don't try it, baby. Don't you never try it."

She didn't try it. Darling Corey wanted to stay alive.

The Man had promised there'd be plenty of bread in this new lay. It would just take time. She'd have to be patient.

Patient.

Well, she'd waited two years since she first met the Man, when he'd told her he'd try it other places first before he'd try it here. A little more waiting wouldn't hurt.

She put the silver bracelet back on and looked at it happily. It was the nicest thing she owned, real silver with "DC" on it in elaborate script. Made just for her, "DC" for Darling Corey. She always wore it.

If the cops just didn't catch on, she thought. The Man had promised her they wouldn't. They didn't at the other places because he'd moved on by the time they started noticing. This time when he moved on he'd take her along.

Oh, well, she wouldn't worry about the cops. Not the regular cops, anyway. They'd take her down to the jail just for a little spat at the Silver Fox or something like that, but she knew that on the big things she could always snow someone like, say, Lloyd Methvin. It was all in knowing how to look at him from under long eyelashes, and how to hold her wrists just right, to look little and sweet and helpless.

There was a new cop in town now, she'd heard, prowling around asking questions about her. Some funny kind of cop who worked in the post office. Lucille had told her about it; Lucille said he'd been here for about a month. Lucille said he was some sort of federal cop. But he couldn't be much to worry about either, even if he was asking questions about her. Who ever heard of a cop working in the post office? He probably wasn't a real cop at all.

Lucille hadn't thought it important enough to mention to the Man, but Darling Corey thought she might better tell him next time she saw him. He always wanted to know things, even if they weren't important.

The only other one who worried her was that girl cop, Cheryl Burroughs. Darling Corey didn't like her nohow. For one thing, being a *girl* cop, she didn't care how little and sweet Darling Corey looked or how pretty she held her arms.

Besides, Darling Corey hadn't forgotten that night two years ago at the Silver Fox when she'd had a lot to drink and just happened to feel like fighting. It had been funny at first, because the other cops were trying to handle her without hurting her. But that girl cop had spotted the little pearl-handled .25 caliber pistol Darling Corey was trying to get to and had grabbed her. She didn't like being grabbed, and she hit the girl cop in the wrist with a wine bottle. The girl cop belted her in the mouth with that little black radio she carried and called her bitch. Darling Corey didn't let nobody call her bitch, but when she tried to hit the girl cop again two other cops grabbed Darling Corey and slung her up hard against a brick wall, not caring anymore whether they hurt her or not.

She'd heard later that the girl cop had gotten a broken wrist in the fight. Even that wasn't much comfort because it took Darling Corey three trips to the dentist to get her teeth fixed, and she had to turn a lot of tricks to pay for that.

She wouldn't try to fight the girl cop again. But she damn sure didn't like her.

Oh, hell, thought Darling Corey, I don't want to think about that now.

She went over and started trying to wake Jimmie. Maybe if she coaxed him into a good mood he'd take her to the dance. After all, putting men in a good mood was her job.

But just as he started to wake up, she glanced out the window. Initially, she wasn't scared by what she saw; from what Lucille had told her, she knew someone would be coming to ask her about those checks, and the Man had told her just what to say to the cops. It would be easy with Cheryl Burroughs there because she could just refuse to talk to Cheryl, and Cheryl wouldn't hit her. Cheryl never hit people unless they tried to hit her first. As for the post office cop, she still hadn't figured out quite what he was, but he wouldn't hit her with Cheryl along. For that matter, if Lucille was right, he wouldn't hit her anyway, because he was a federal cop, and federal cops didn't—

She had gotten that far along telling Jimmie who had driven up when he snatched a gun and ran to the window. "The goddamn feds!" he was yelling as he fired the first shot and then ran back inside the room to snatch out more guns that Darling Corey hadn't even known he'd brought.

Darling Corey was badly frightened. As Cheryl was saying to Allen, this type of shooting wasn't her speed. She checked the .25 caliber automatic she always carried in her purse and grabbed a box of bullets out of her dressing table drawer. Then, seeing that Jimmie was totally occupied at the window, she snatched five bills from the roll of hundreds he carried. Any more than that and he might notice—if, that is, he managed to get out alive. Just as Jimmie picked up the shotgun, Darling Corey ran down the back stairs.

Looking after Jimmie was fine, but surely she wasn't expected to stay in something like this! With her own pistol, and five hundred dollars of Jimmie's bread, Darling Corey ran.

***

• *14* •

Six blocks from the yard where Jimmie Pitts now lay dead, Darling Corey hailed a Southside Cab. "Where to, Darling Corey?"

"Oh, around," Darling Corey said vaguely.

"Now look, baby, I ain't takin' no play for pay, my ol' lady, she—"

"You cain't afford me nohow," Darling Corey said contemptuously. "I got plenty bread. Just drive me 'round for a while."

"Lemme see yo' bread."

Darling Corey held up one of the bills and then stuffed it back inside her dress. "Now drive me 'round."

"Okay, baby, anywheah you wanna go."

In the back of the cab, Darling Corey adjusted her make-up. She smoothed on dark green eye shadow heavy from eyelash to painted-on eyebrows, put on new copper-red lipstick, thick rose blusher, musky cologne. Luckily, the glued-on eyelashes and the long, lemon-yellow fingernails had stood up to her panicked flight. In the mirror, her face looked back at her, light brown skin with rosy cheeks under high cheekbones, framed by a fluffy Afro. She looked the same as always; nobody would guess she'd been fleeing a shooting. "Now take me to the Pine Tree Motel," Darling Corey directed.

"You gots the dough, takes you wheah you wanna go." He swung the cab in a rather unsteady U-turn and headed down Petroleum Street.

Three blocks farther on, Darling Corey leaned forward. "Hey, Berry, stop here at the liquor store." There, feeling reasonably sure she would not be taken to task for spending Jimmie's bread, she bought a fifth of Black Velvet. She hoped the Man hadn't needed Jimmie too bad, because judging from the number of sirens she was hearing, whether Jimmie was alive or dead, the cops had him now.

She paid the fare and then, relaxing with a loose joint she'd found at the bottom of her bag, tipped Berry a dollar and promised him more if he'd bring her a dime bag. She thought, regretfully, of her abandoned stash. But maybe they wouldn't find it. It was reasonably well hidden.

With Berry's fervent promise to deliver the dime bag, she checked into the motel and paid for two days' stay. By the time that money was used up, she'd have had time to reach the Man and find out what to do next. And maybe, if she was really lucky, the cops wouldn't find the hidey-hole where the rest of Jimmie's roll was.

You don't need a search warrant to search a crime scene.

The door to Darling Corey's room was wide, which saved the trouble of kicking it open. Sergeant Hall brought the camera up from the car and handed it to his newest detective, Lloyd Methvin, who had turned out to be a surprisingly good photographer. "Photos all around," he directed, "and don't touch anything."

FBI agent Steve Karney said, "Can we just have prints from your negatives? Save me the trouble of taking the same set of photos."

"Something better save you the trouble," the other agent said drily. "You left our camera in Marshall. I was wondering if you'd noticed yet." Karney grinned.

"Yeah, sure," Hall said.

Methvin took overlapping photos from the front door around each room, showing the unmade bed, the liquor bottles, the roach clip, the remains of carryout chicken boxes and hamburger meals. He took an extra close-up of the rifle and the pistol lying by the front window and of the open boxes of shotgun shells, .30-06 bullets, and .357 bullets on the floor between the window and the bed. Then he went to the window and took another photo looking back at the door. Catching a fresh view of the dresser, he whistled. "Damn, look-a there!" he said, and took a closeup of the roll of hundreds fluttering in the breeze.

After the photos came fingerprints, and only then, with the room thoroughly spread with black powder, did they begin searching. After Methvin's discovery of the rest of the money, along with the wrappers that told them it came from the Kilgore bank robbery two weeks earlier, finding Darling Corey's stash came as an anti-climax.

The phone rang in Cheryl's little rented house, and she got off the couch and reached for it. "Hello? Hi, Allen, how are you?"

"A little sore but otherwise okay. The ant bites hurt worse than anything else. How about you?"

"I'm not even sore, just crabby, except I have the grandfather of all headaches. I have my stereo turned up loud so I can't hear the hammers in my head."

"Yeah, I can hear it over the phone," Allen said. "Why bagpipes?"

"They fit my mood," Cheryl answered, and from her tone of voice Allen could visualize her shrug.

"If I came over and brought a bottle," he asked, "would you have anything I could mix it with?"

"I don't drink. But I think I've got some 7-Up." She tried not to sound too inviting.

"I'll bring some more in case you don't. Be right there." Ignoring the lack of invitation, he hung up before she had time to ask what he planned on driving. They couldn't have gotten his windshield fixed that fast. He might have gotten a rented car, she guessed, and started picking up the living room.

"Who's the picture?" Allen asked an hour later, gesturing lazily at the wall with the glass in his hand.

"That's Holly. My daughter."

"Your daughter!"

Cheryl got up and headed toward the kitchen. "Yes. My daughter. A long time ago, six years ago when I was twenty-two, I—made a little mistake. I didn't see any reason to compound the mistake by marrying a man I by then detested. That's Holly. She's five. She's spending the month with her father and I hate it, because he's no good and I'm always afraid she's not safe there, but he's a friend of the judge and there's nothing I can do about it. So, as I said, that's my daughter. Now, what do you want to say about it?"

"She's a very pretty little girl. What do you expect me to say?" Allen sat up straighter and lit a cigarette. "I didn't ask for your life history; I just asked who she is."

"Excuse me," Cheryl said, turning back toward him with another glass of 7-Up. "I told you I'm being crabby tonight."

"Be as crabby as you want to, as long as you shoot straight. Just don't be mad at me. Hey, I've asked your sergeant for the loan of you for the rest of the week, and I'll probably want to extend it on into some of next week. I hope that's okay with you. But I want to tell you, just so you'll know if you happen to wonder, that I'm unattached. I've had a sort of unpleasant divorce, and I'm not looking for anything permanent, at least not yet. But I like you a lot, and I thought maybe we could have a little fun, you know? But only if you feel like it."

"I didn't ask for your life history, either," Cheryl answered. "No, I don't want anything permanent either. Or temporary. Or anything else."

"Just friends, then?"

Cheryl eyed him, silently, and then said abruptly, "So you're divorced. How many children is your ex bringing up by herself?"

Allen had been opening a package of cigarettes; he paused and looked over at her quickly, his eyes the hardest she'd ever seen them, a muscle in his face twitching. "None," he said in a carefully even voice. "Lisa didn't want children. She was afraid they'd ruin her pretty figure. Yours doesn't seem to have suffered."

"You didn't see me when I was pregnant."

His hard eyes seemed to soften. "I wish I had," he returned. "I'll bet you looked great."

She smiled slowly, the pounding headache receding a little. "Not really," she answered. "All right, you want to be friends, we'll be friends. But that's all I want. Probably it'll be all I'll ever want, from you or anybody else." She looked at him again. "As a friend, I guess you'll do. But don't push it."

"Okay, friend," he said, and stood up and solemnly shook her hand, an irrepressible grin hovering around the corners of his mouth. "But if you happen to change your mind, remember that I'm around. Still going to work with me?"

"I wouldn't miss it. After all, it's *interesting* riding with you."

Allen laughed aloud. "That it is," he agreed. "All right, give me another drink and I'll go home and get some rest like a good little boy." On the last word he started to chuckle again. "Oh, lord," he said, shaking his head, "I wouldn't make a very good romantic hero anyway, would I? I'm forty-two years old and getting bald already—"

"You are not bald," Cheryl interrupted.

"Getting bald, I said, see the top of my head? And I'm shaped exactly like a teddy bear."

"But such a pleasant teddy bear," Cheryl said lightly. "And I make a great romantic heroine, right? I crawl around on my little tum-tum under cars and get all dirty and besides that, I shoot people. And everybody knows all female cops who aren't just crossing guards are horse-faced."

Allen looked at Cheryl. Her 115 pounds were very pleasantly distributed over her five feet of height. Her brown eyes didn't need any accent, and now, in the evening, the long brown hair she usually pinned on top of her head was in two fat braids. Allen lifted one eyebrow. "Yeah?" he said and stood up. "Forget about that second drink, lady, I've got to go."

· *Two* ·

It started out to be a nobody-knows-nothing and the complainant doesn't want to be contacted kind of day. Cheryl got into the office at seven-thirty, ten minutes early even for muster, and Sergeant Hall instantly handed her the keys to car 16. "Seventeen is in the shop," he told her. "Four-to-twelve bent it a little."

"Rat shit," Cheryl said. "Is the air conditioning fixed on—"

"No, the air conditioning isn't fixed on 16. In case you haven't noticed, it's on the fritz in here again, too."

"I noticed. Uh, what do you want me to do with these car keys?"

"Report of a child abuse, complainant doesn't—"

"Want to be contacted," she finished for him. "Complainant always doesn't want to be contacted on a child abuse. All right, all right, where is it at?"

And sometimes reports, even anonymous reports, of child abuse are legitimate; Cheryl had walked into houses where diapers hadn't been changed in two days and four-year-olds were eating moldy bread while Mamas were passed out drunk. But in this house she found Linnea Watson, nineteen, whose husband had just entered the Army, changing the diaper on a colicky six-week-old girl while a twelve-month-old boy howled steadily. Linnea, who was very pretty and very black, looked ready to drop. "They're both in diapers," she told Cheryl, "and every time Janie wakes up, Craig wakes up too, and I can't get any rest at all and—who called you anyway?"

"I wish I knew," Cheryl said, surveying dishes in the kitchen sink. She'd already had a glimpse of a clean but nearly empty refrigerator. "Look, would you be offended if I asked the Department of Family and Children's Services to see if they can get you some help for a week or two?"

"Is that welfare?"

"Well, sort of, but—"

Linnea looked around at her husband's picture. "Chris wouldn't like that. No, I'll manage okay. Janie's got to start sleeping through the night sometime or other. I remember Craig was like this when he was first born."

"I'll check back with you in a few days, then, all right?" On her way back to the car, Cheryl noticed a woman with tight grey curls and apple cheeks standing across the street watering roses and avidly watching the front door of Linnea Watson's duplex. On impulse, Cheryl walked over to her. "Hi," she said, "I'm Detective Burroughs. Somebody called me out here on an absolutely false report of child abuse in that duplex, and I've been in there talking to that poor girl. With her husband in boot camp and two children in diapers, she really does need some help bad. Do you know of any nice motherly woman in the neighborhood who could offer to look after those babies for a few hours so she could get some rest?"

"Well—uh—" The woman was clearly caught off guard. "I could go over, now that you mention it. I really didn't know—she just moved in there a couple of weeks ago, you see, with no husband, and—I mean I didn't know—you see—"

I see, Cheryl thought. I see it was too much trouble for you to go knock on the door and say, "I'm your neighbor." It was easier to pick up the phone and call the police.

She had just started the car again when the dispatcher said, "Report of a stolen CB radio at 702 Hite. Car 16, can you handle it?"

He hadn't locked his truck. Well, no, he hadn't shut the vent window either—and just why in the hell couldn't Cheryl get any fingerprints? Goddamn women police think they don't have to do nothing. I seen on *Barney Miller*—

Report of a child playing with a gun, complainant doesn't want to be contacted. Why couldn't uniform division handle? Well, the beat car was having a break right now.

Cheryl hadn't eaten breakfast this morning. Her mouth felt dry and she was, she noticed, beginning to feel distinctly sorry for herself.

The child was eight years old. His mom had gone to get her hair done. His dad worked in a building downtown; his dad was a lawyer.

Cheryl baby-sat until Dad's secretary got there.

Shit, Cheryl thought. Rat shit.

That isn't ladylike. Ladies don't go around saying rat shit. If I don't quit saying rat shit, Holly will pick it up. Can't send a kid to kindergarten saying rat shit.

Car 16, report of a—

Rat shit.

It wasn't until eleven o'clock that the dispatcher said, "Car 16, can you twenty-five for a twenty-nine?"

That sounds idiotic, Cheryl thought. Twenty-five means come to the PD, twenty-nine means meet another officer (and I hope to goodness it's Allen), but I wonder what it sounds like to people listening to scanners? Oh, well, they're probably used to it all.

I am about to work myself into an attack of the giggles, she told herself sternly, realizing that it was the aftermath of the shock of the day before and that she probably should have stayed out another day.

She drove into the unpaved parking lot in back of city hall. Entering the basement that housed the police station, she hung the keys of car 16 on a cup hook behind Sergeant Hall's desk. "Hi," she said to Allen.

"Hi," he said. "You want to go help me talk to some more people? Your sergeant says it's okay."

"Yeah. You want me to take along a riot gun?"

"No, I've talked to these people before. How come you took off your bandage? Did the doctor say you could?"

"I didn't ask the doctor. It felt silly. Did you leave yours on? Hey, look, I'm not going anywhere without this radio today whether you like it or not. Kathy, I'll be ten-six the rest of the day—Allen, slow down!"

On the steps outside, he asked, "When did the air conditioning break down? I thought I'd smother waiting for you in there."

"Pity Kathy, she's stuck in it all day. It does that about once a month. But my car is just as bad. Look at this!" She held out one damp strand of hair that had worked free from the pinned-up braids. "I think I'll get it all cut off."

"My own car," he said, "is too damn air-conditioned right now. But just wait 'til you get in this one I rented. It'll freeze you right out."

"When will yours be fixed?"

"They promised tomorrow. Probably the day after. We're going to talk to Lucille Brantley at the Super Launderette at twelve-thirty, but I thought you might want some lunch first. I didn't have any breakfast. Did you?"

"Didn't wake up in time. Maybe that's why I've felt so cross all morning."

He drove for one block in complete silence and then said, "Cheryl, that scared the hell out of me yesterday. Nobody ever really shot at me before. Somebody started to a couple of times, but nobody actually did it. Could you tell how scared I was?"

"No, I was too busy worrying about how scared *I* was," Cheryl answered. "I was scared I'd get hurt, and I was scared you'd get hurt, and I was scared I'd chicken."

"Were you really? I never even thought of that."

"Never thought I'd chicken?"

"Never thought *I* would. Never thought you would either, for that matter. Actually, I don't think I even thought of thinking about that. Speaking of chicken, want some?"

"I guess. . . . Allen?"

"Yeah?"

"We killed a man yesterday. You and I. We did."

"That's right," Allen said soberly, pulling under a sign that said "Victoria's Fried Chicken Georgia Style."

"And you know what's awful about it?"

"No, what?"

"I don't even care. I really don't. I tried to care, and I just don't."

"Yes, you do," Allen said. "If you didn't, you wouldn't be talking the way you are right now."

"Do you care?"

"Of course I care." He paused in the act of getting out of the car. "He wasn't worth anything to anybody, and he was a criminal, and he was trying to kill us. But he was alive and now he's not. Yes, I care, but I realize we had no choice. I care, but I don't feel guilty. Why, do you?"

She sat quite still in the cold car, the long bullet cut across her right upper arm clearly visible in her sleeveless blouse. "I don't know," she said finally. "I need to think about it some more. I don't know right now, Allen. Don't look at me like that. Why are you looking at me like that?" She put the shirt jacket on to hide the shoulder holster.

"Like what? I'm just looking and listening to what you say." But unusually for him, the grin was a little forced. "Come on, let's eat, we've got places to go and things to do."

"Right." Inside she said, "No, you don't, we're riding together but you didn't take me to raise."

"Okay," Allen said meekly, paying for his own lunch.

"What are we talking to—" Cheryl glanced around at unfamiliar faces. "To the person you mentioned about?"

"To see if she knows where, ah, another person is, for starters," Allen said. "Then too, I kind of think she knows what's going on. She's been feeding me a little information all along, and if I keep digging she keeps giving me a little more and a little more. Only problem is that she's more scared of whoever she's working for than she is of me. She's asked me twice how she's supposed to know I'm not from the Man, and you I guess she knows."

"Though I don't guarantee how much of an advantage that will be," Cheryl said and concentrated on chicken and slaw. "I've jailed her twice."

A minute later Allen said gloomily, "Of course, she's not going to tell me who this man she's scared of is. And that's what I really need to know."

"You don't figure there's any way you can talk her into telling you?"

"I know darn well I can't. She's scared. I mean she is really scared."

In the dark, wearing a wig, a short skirt, and high-heeled sandals, Lucille Brantley might look enticing to a not-very-particular man who was maybe half drunk anyway.

But in the bright sunlight that came through the laundromat window, Lucille Brantley, wearing twenty-seven braids, a torn overblouse, dirty shorts and no shoes, was a rather astonishing mess. She smelled of gardenia cologne, sweat, and the aftermath of last night's activities, and the purple nail polish was chipping off her fingernails and toenails. She slapped half-heartedly at a whining two-year-old who was clinging to her leg. "You gon' gi' me some money?" she asked Allen.

"I might," Allen drawled, "if you've got anything to say I want to hear."

Lucille cast a hostile glance at Cheryl. "You gon' put me in jail?"

"Not today," Cheryl said.

"You puts me in jail last week."

"You rolled a drunk last week."

"I ain' rolled no—"

"Never mind, never mind," Allen interrupted hastily. "Let's don't talk about that. Nobody's putting you in jail right now. We just want to talk to you, understand?''

"You axes me what you wants to know."

"Where's Darling Corey?''

(Not, Cheryl noticed, "Do you know where she is?''—a question that would call for a no answer—but, "Where is she?'')

The result, however, was about the same. "I don' know. She stay over there on the corner."

"I know, but she's gone somewhere else right now.''

"Did you tried the Pine Tree Motel?''

"She's not there either.''

"Then I doesn't know.''

"Who does she work for?''

Lucille abandoned her attempt at formality and laughed contemptuously. "You don' know much, you think somebody run Darling Corey. Don' nobody run that girl.''

"I didn't mean that. The checks—''

"Don' know nothin' about no checks." Lucille suddenly busied herself with the washing machine, which needed no attention whatever.

Allen took a twenty and his business card out of his pocket and looked at them musingly. "Somebody told me you knew something.''

"Then somebody done tol' you a lie. I tol' you, I don' know nothing. I don' wants to talk to you no more." She turned her back to him.

"Okay, here's my phone number in case you change your mind.''

"Don' want your phone number. I don' know nothing.''

"You think there's any chance she really doesn't know?'' Cheryl asked in the car.

"She may not know where Darling Corey is right now, but she damn well knows who's behind all those checks,'' Allen answered. "I've got a couple in my desk drawer that she cashed herself.''

"Can you prove it?''

"Not yet, but I will when I want to. But unfortunately all that'll get me is a guilty plea from her, in State court at that, because they don't let us take a first offender into federal court unless we can show it's really a big deal. So arresting her won't do any good. I need to know who's behind it. Damn it, I want to talk to Darling Corey. I need to know if Jimmie Pitts was imported on purpose or if he just happened to be here.''

"That would be quite a coincidence, wouldn't it?'' Cheryl asked.

Allen shrugged. "Coincidences happen. I just want to know. Let's go by my office. I need to see what else has come in."

Cheryl waited as Allen leafed through notes on his desk. "Damn, there's another one," he said half to himself.

"Another what? Let me guess. Another check."

"Another check. Cheryl?"

"Yep?"

"Where is Four Mile Road? This check was supposed to have been mailed to Four Mile Road. I thought I knew this county by now, but—"

"In one month, you can scarcely be expected to know where Four Mile Road is," Cheryl answered. "Go west on Ford's Landing Road to Carter's Grocery and turn left at Carter's Grocery and go four miles and turn left again."

"Let me guess. It's Four Mile Road because it's four miles from Carter's Grocery."

"No."

"Then why?" Allen demanded. "Look, I'm a city boy. Don't expect me to understand this kind of thing."

"Because it's four miles from the grist mill that used to be where Carter's Grocery is now," Cheryl explained.

"When was the grist mill there?"

"Oh, about 1870."

"Thank heaven for local cops," Allen answered. "How am *I* supposed to know *that?* Okay, then let's go out past the former site of this defunct grist mill."

"Where was the check cashed?" Cheryl asked. "Carter's?"

Allen turned the check, encased in its plastic sleeve to protect any possible fingerprints, over again. "No. Its second endorser is somebody named John Arnold. Know him?"

"Do I! We're going to get a straight story for once," Cheryl said. "And you'll like John Arnold. Let's go there first."

John Arnold was six feet two with the build of a professional boxer. The build was fairly noticeable, as he was standing behind the counter of Arnold's Superette in black slacks and a rather snug-fitting white T-shirt. He was as close to being truly black as any person Allen had ever seen, and he grinned broadly at the two entering the store. "Hello, Cheryl," he said, in a cultured baritone. "Who's your friend?"

"John, this is Allen Conyers. He's the new postal inspector."

"Are you assigned here?" John demanded, reaching across the counter to shake hands very firmly. "God knows we've been needing one."

"Yeah, that was getting pretty obvious," Allen said ruefully. "One of the inspectors in Dallas was threatening to move over here."

"Any idea how long you'll be here? You fellows don't seem to stay put long, and I kind of thought they'd been closing all the little offices."

"They decided to reopen this one," Allen said, "and they wanted to put somebody in it who'd already worked the larger cities and was maybe headed for retirement, so as to maybe keep me here."

"You didn't mention that to me," Cheryl said.

"When have I had time?" Allen asked her. "No," he added to John, "I don't know the rationale behind opening an office here when the ones in places like Tyler and Amarillo are closed up, but I guess somebody somewhere had some reason."

"Somebody somewhere usually does," John agreed wryly.

"You speak as one who knows," Allen remarked. "How come? I mean, I don't usually expect storekeepers to—"

John grinned. "I retired a bird colonel, Army intelligence—quit snickering, Cheryl—and came back here to run my daddy's store. Didn't want to let it go. It's been in the family since 1872."

"I owe you one for that, Cheryl," Allen said. "John, she set me up real good. All she told me about you was that we'd get a straight story from you. I sort of expected—" He stopped, looking puzzled. "I don't know what I did expect."

"Somebody like my daddy, probably," John said, "who also would have given you a straight story, only—shall we say—with a little less finesse. All right. Straight story on what?"

"This," Allen said, and handed him the sleeved check. "It was passed in this store."

"Gwendolyn Munson—yeah, I remember. She was a fairly young woman, said she was getting a widow's pension from Social Security because she had a child in school."

"You didn't have any problem about cashing the check?"

"No, she had—well, since you're here I assume it wasn't, but she had what looked like adequate identification."

"Which was?"

"Texas driver's license, the correct number of digits. Photo and all.

Look, for Pete's sake, I wrote the DL on the back of the check, right here."

"You did," Allen agreed, "and we ran it, and it came back listed to a Carl Embree in Port Aransas."

"Then it was a damn good imitation," John said, "because I'm observant, and it looked legit to me."

"Any other identification? Credit card or anything like that?"

John laughed wryly and gestured outside to the unpaved street and the ramshackle shotgun houses. "My customers don't have credit cards. She had a food stamp identification card. Also forged?"

"Also forged. Would you recognize her if you saw her again?"

"I doubt it," John said. "She was dressed up fit to kill, nice wig, sharp dress, high-heel sandals, lots of make-up. If she was to come in here today in shorts and barefoot, plaited or nappy hair, no make-up—no, I wouldn't know her. Dressed the same, yeah, I might."

"But the ID did look real?"

"It looked damn real," John answered. "It looked perfect."

"Okay," Allen said. "Well, thanks."

"But no use, right?"

"I wouldn't say that," Allen said. "It bears out what I was beginning to think anyway. We've got locals at the bottom but we've got pros, or at least semi-pros, at the top."

"Did any other checks come through my store?"

"Yeah," Allen said, "some did. Not knowing you, I didn't see any sense in bringing the others along until I saw whether it was any use talking to you. I've got seven or eight that hit you."

"Seven or eight? I hope to God my theft insurance covers forgeries!"

"I hope so, too," Allen agreed, "because they do mount up."

"And I've been trying to locate one of those gadgets that puts fingerprints on the backs of checks," John added gloomily, "and nobody seems to know who handles them around here."

"You mean like Identiseal? I'll see if I can find somebody," Cheryl said.

"I'd appreciate it." He paused to ring up a packet of cigarettes handed him by a small, round-bellied boy dressed only in dirty yellow shorts but shook his head at the note the child handed him. "You tell your mama she knows better than that."

"I done tole her, but she say try anyways."

"You tell her I say if she wants beer, she comes to get it," John said. When the boy left, he turned back to Allen. "Of course, selling the cigarettes to the kid is a technical violation, but it's one of those things everybody does. But you understand what I mean about recognizing her?"

"Yeah, it makes sense," Allen agreed.

"But I'll do what I can," John added. "You want to get with me tomorrow about those other checks?"

"Tomorrow or another day. I may see if I can round up some pictures for you to look at first."

"I'll do what I can. But it may not be much."

"Thanks again," Allen said.

In the car again, Cheryl remarked, "Last year a couple of punk kids who thought he would be a pushover tried to stick him up. John's got a .45 under the counter. One of the punks was buried; the other spent six weeks in the hospital before going on to prison."

"Good for John. Have you known him all your life?"

"Sort of. He's just been retired for two years, but his mother worked for my mother, and I'd met his daddy. So I'd see pictures of John and see him when he was home on leave. Well! What do we do now?"

Allen looked at his watch. "I guess we've still got time to go to Four Mile Road."

But there was not much to be learned on Four Mile Road. Gwendolyn Munson, plump, seventy-three, and still with some of the lilt of the Wales she had left at eleven in her voice, had been on a visit to her daughter when her Social Security check was put in her mailbox. Arriving home on the third of April, she found its torn envelope on her front porch. By the time she'd reported the theft, the check had already been cashed.

"I'm supposed to be off duty now," Allen said. "Not that I'm habitually a clock watcher, but I do need a break. Do you have to go back in to check out?"

"No, but I do have to go get my car eventually. But I promised my mother I'd drop by for a few minutes. Look, she lives just down the road, would you mind?"

"Glad to," Allen said.

"Because really, it would be silly for you to drive me back into town so that I could get my car and drive right back out here. Sure you don't mind? It won't be long. But she got a little shook up when she saw us on the news last night, and she wanted to be sure I'm really okay."

"Tell me where to turn."

The house wasn't as old as John Arnold's grocery store, but it was old enough to have a water well with a bucket on a pulley on the big, dim, screened-in front porch. "The house is on city water now," Cheryl explained as they entered, "but the well water is super for drinking."

Inside, Cheryl's mother eyed Allen with a transparent eagerness. "And you're dating Cheryl?" she asked hopefully after Cheryl walked down the hall.

"We're friends," Allen said.

"Oh," she responded, apparently rather let down. "Well, it was nice of you to drop by, anyways. Could I get you something? A glass of tea? Some buttermilk? It surely is hot for this early in the year!"

Allen wondered how she could tell, with the air conditioner so high he was half-expecting his teeth to start chattering. But he accepted her fourth offer, a cup of Sanka. "And I know Cheryl will want one," she added.

"One what?" Cheryl asked, returning in a bulky white sweater.

"A cup of Sanka," Allen said. Looking at the kitchen door, he added very softly, "She offered me iced drinks first before she got to hot ones. Good grief, I'm about to freeze!"

"The first thing I always do when I get here is go after this sweater," Cheryl answered. "Winter is when you want something cold to drink here. Then the living room stays about ninety degrees, but I think right now it's about sixty. I can't figure out why it doesn't kill her to get out and work half the day in the garden in the heat and then come back in to this refrigerator, but she thrives on it. But you're not a coffee drinker?" she asked curiously. "Mama keeps Sanka for me, but usually nobody else wants it."

"No, I never did start drinking coffee," Allen answered. "I always figured if I didn't get in the habit of it, then I wouldn't miss it if I didn't have time for it."

"Makes sense," Cheryl said.

Twenty minutes later, when Cheryl announced that no she couldn't eat another slice of pie and they really had to go, her mother exclaimed, "But you can't go before you see who Charlotte's new boyfriend is!"

"Has Charlotte got another new boyfriend?" Cheryl asked sharply. "You better watch that girl, Mama, or she'll be in as much trouble in high school as I was in college."

Mrs. Burroughs glanced quickly at Allen and then said, "Now, Cheryl, I don't think so. If you'd dated more in high school and college, you'd have known better how to handle yourself when situations did arise."

"And yes, Allen knows what we're talking about," Cheryl added with a trace of bitterness. "He saw Holly's picture yesterday. Look, we don't have time—"

"But here she comes now!" Mrs. Burroughs crowed.

Charlotte was taller than Cheryl by at least four inches. Her hair was ash blond where Cheryl's was brown. With the same brown eyes and clear dark tan that Cheryl had, she looked thoroughly theatrical. "Oh, my, Cheryl, is this your boyfriend?" she cooed in a strangely affected voice. "Cheryl, Cheryl's boyfriend, this is my boyfriend Waymon Thomas. He's a reporter."

"Hello, Waymon," Cheryl said with dignity, although her face betrayed so much discomfort that Allen felt an urge to spank Charlotte. "It's interesting to meet you, finally," Cheryl was saying. "Charlotte, Waymon, my friend Allen Conyers."

"H'lo, Allen," Waymon said, reaching out to shake hands. "Hi, Cheryl. Didn't I hear you're a cop now?"

"Oh, wow, look at the brain! She's wearing a shoulder holster and he guesses she's a cop! What an asshole! Anyway, Cheryl's the only sister I've got, and if she tries to be a cop at *me*, I'll paste her one."

"Deborah Charlotte!"

"Mama, I'm just too hot and tired!" Charlotte wailed and sank into a chair. A whiteness edged the corners of her mouth, and there was a strange, wild look in her eyes.

"Oh, honey, let me get you some tea!"

Waymon stood, looking awkward and a little defensive, as Cheryl said, "Mama, we'd better go." She pitched her sweater across the arm of a chair. "I'm sorry," she told Allen outside, "she gets like that about once in six months. The doctor thinks it might be psychomotor epilepsy. She'll be okay tomorrow, but for some reason she's always worse when I'm around."

Waymon, who had followed them outside, said, "I didn't know what to do. I picked her up this morning and we went out to the park swimming, and then all of a sudden she started acting just flaky."

"Thanks for bringing her home," Cheryl said. "We do have to go now."

"Well, it was nice meeting you," Waymon said. "Allen, are you a cop too?"

"Postal inspector," Allen answered.

"Postal inspector. Oh," Waymon said vaguely, "that's interesting. I didn't know there was one around here." He looked at their car, put his hands in his pockets, and drifted back toward the house, pausing to stand and stare at the roses.

Turning, Allen said, "I'm glad you told me what was wrong. I'd hate to think she was like that all the time. Now! We are off duty—at least, I have to go sometime after midnight to check a rural post office substation, because we're having some thefts out of it, but I'm off duty until then. Now I want you to do something for me. There's a movie I want to see, and I hate to go to the movies alone. Besides that, it's at the drive-in, and I don't really want to be thought of as a man who goes to the drive-in by himself. I promise not to be a pest. I really want to see this movie."

Cheryl laughed. "Put that way, how can I refuse?" She slammed her car door.

Allen walked around to get in the car and added, "Dinner first?"

"Okay," Cheryl agreed. "Dinner first, after I go home and take about a two-hour nap. But Allen—"

"I know. Just friends. But can't we go places with our friends? If you can't stand owing me, you can cook me dinner one day next week."

"You're on," Cheryl said.

At ten o'clock, Allen stretched and moved over toward her. "It's not comfortable trying to watch a movie from behind a steering wheel."

"Probably not," Cheryl agreed. But she stiffened a moment later. "Please don't put your arm around me."

"Okay," he said meekly and moved back behind the steering wheel. At intermission he asked, "Cheryl, will you tell me why?"

"Why what?"

"We're both adults. You've got a child; I've been married, and it's not my doing I don't have kids. I know we agreed to just be friends, but I didn't figure my just putting my arm around you could possibly be misconstrued.''

"I didn't misconstrue it."

"No, I don't think you did. You completely disliked it; you practically shuddered. Why, Cheryl? Is it something I've said or done?''

"It's nothing to do with you."

"I mean, you don't owe me, there's no reason why you should want me to put my arm around you, it's just—''

"I said it's nothing to do with you." After a minute she added, "I just hate being touched by anybody at all. I'm not gay if that's what you're thinking now. If I wanted anybody to touch me it would probably be you, but I just hate being touched.''

"Cheryl, did he rape you? Holly's father? Did he rape you?''

"He told me he could make me stop hating to be touched. I was young enough to believe him. Now I hate it even more." She wasn't crying, not visibly, but Allen could hear a stifled sob.

"God, Cheryl," Allen said, "I feel so damn helpless. I want to comfort you, and I don't even know how to try to comfort you without touching you. Cheryl, Cheryl, can't you believe I'd never do anything to hurt you?''

"He said that, too. Allen, I didn't mean that the way it sounded. I know you wouldn't hurt me. I just hate being touched, that's all. It's nothing to do with you. And you don't have to try to comfort me.''

"I know that, but you're hurt, and I—Cheryl, all right, we haven't known each other long, but we've been through too much together for me to see you hurt without caring. Won't you at least tell me what happened?''

"I've never told anybody that."

"Then trust me."

"I do trust you."

"Then tell me, Cheryl."

"If I do, I trust you more than I've ever trusted anybody." She dashed tears out of her face. "All right. Cops see a lot of things." She was curled as far over on the right side of the car as she could get. "I've seen a lot that you haven't. Allen, what do you suppose is the most under-reported major crime in this country?''

"I don't know. Probably rape."

"No. It's child molestation. And a rape usually happens just once, but child molestation can go on for years—and years—and years—and years, and nobody ever notices it, and nobody ever stops it, because all anybody ever sees is how *affectionate* uncle is with his sister's little girl!"

"Was it your uncle, Cheryl?"

"Yes. And it doesn't do any good to tell me not to feel guilty because I know it wasn't my fault, but I did feel guilty and I still do. And I didn't know who to tell or what to do. He was killed in a car wreck when I was fifteen, and I cried then because I felt guilty to be so relieved when everybody else was grieving. But since then—I just hate being touched."

"Cheryl, hasn't any male in your life ever held you without trying to do anything else?"

"Not that I can remember."

"Your father?"

"He never held me. I don't think he liked children. He died when I was twelve, anyway."

"A grandfather?"

"One I never saw. The other died when I was five."

"Before you were five? Didn't he ever hold you in his lap?"

"He might have. I don't remember."

Allen took a deep breath. "Did you think of seeing a doctor?"

"I did see one when I was in college. I couldn't even stand to get in a car with a guy. I didn't tell her what the reason was, but I think she pretty well guessed. She told me about something called aversion therapy or something like that. She said if I'd ride around in a car with a guy, whether I liked it or not, eventually I'd get to where that wouldn't bother me. And then I should get some guy to hug me for a long time, and so on."

"It must have started working. You asked to ride with me."

"Yeah. But it was Holly's daddy I asked to hold me. Since then I haven't been willing to trust a man that far." She stopped, startled, apparently hearing her own words, and looked at him. "All right, Allen, he did rape me. Yes. He did. And I told the police in the town where it happened. They didn't believe me. They called it a lover's quarrel because everybody knew I'd been dating him. And he thought it was funny; he thought it shouldn't matter any more to me than it would to—to Darling Corey. Nobody will ever rape me again, not and live to laugh about it."

"Is that why you're a cop?"

"Partly, I guess," she answered. "You can't get a pistol permit in Texas. So the only way a woman can carry a gun legally is to be a cop."

"You told me you trust me. Do you?"

"I guess so," she said reluctantly.

"Then give me your hand a minute," he said quietly and guided it. "That's a part of my body, Cheryl," he said. "That's all it is, no more and no less. It's not a weapon to use to hurt you or anybody else." He released her hand and she jerked it away. He continued, still quietly, "It's like it is right now because you're an attractive woman and I care a lot about you. But if you ever touch me there again it will be your choice. I promise you I'll never again ask you to. All I'm asking you to do is let me put my arm around you while we watch this show. And I'm forty-two years old, Cheryl, and you flatter me most excessively if you think I can't keep my arm around an attractive woman for two hours without losing control."

Unwillingly, Cheryl laughed. "And that's another thing," she said. "I don't guess I'll ever know—what there is to lose control about."

"Cheryl, you make me want to cry."

"Don't pity me!"

"I don't pity you. I—Cheryl, yesterday, when we were under the car, you thought for a minute I was hit bad. How did that make you feel?"

"Awful."

"All right. You've been hurt a lot more than a bullet could hurt because it's a hurt that hasn't healed. I care because I care about you."

"But you might hold me forever and I'd never like it."

"That might be true."

"You don't have forever to wait."

"No, I don't," he agreed. "I don't know how long I'll live, but I have every reason to expect to be in this town however long that is. No, I don't know that you'll ever feel comfortable about being loved, but maybe I can help you to accept somebody caring about you. And that's not pity, Cheryl."

"Okay, but I don't think you'll enjoy holding onto me and knowing I'm miserable."

"Maybe not," Allen agreed. She leaned back against him, not relaxed and not secure, and he put his arm around her very carefully, making sure his hand didn't go past her shoulder. Gradually, as she became absorbed in the movie, some of the tension began to leave her. Then he, too, began to relax, although he was careful to warn her if he started to shift position.

After a while she added, "Allen, Uncle Jack loved me. He was just all mixed up in his ways of thinking. He really didn't mean to hurt me, and he'd have been awfully sorry if he'd known he did."

"And I think that makes it much worse in the long run," Allen said softly. "Because if a wild-eyed monster out of an alley attacks you, you can go to the ones who love you for comfort. But if the ones who love you *are* the ones who attack you, then where is there to go, and how can you trust anyone else no matter how much they love you?"

"I think you've been hurt, too, to understand that," Cheryl said.

"I've been hurt," Allen answered. "It's too recent for me to discuss it yet without coming apart. When I can, I'll tell you."

"That bad? Was it your wife?"

"Yes. And I'll tell you this. I know—I know absolutely from some things you've already done that even if you tried to hurt me you couldn't hurt me the way she did. Not that you'd ever want to."

There was a long silence, during which Allen did not watch the movie and was fairly sure Cheryl didn't either. Finally she said, "Allen?"

"Yeah?"

"Do you—you haven't known me long enough to love me."

"Probably not. So don't let's say I do. Just good friends for now. Right?"

"Right."

But inwardly he rejoiced because then she settled, very cautiously, back into his embrace. It was almost the end of the movie before he said unwillingly, "Sit up now, Cheryl, and let me get a cigarette." He tried to get his lighter out of his pocket, dropped it, couldn't find it, and resignedly turned on the ignition and pushed in the lighter in the dash.

"Why do you want a cigarette now?"

"Just do."

"It's only the second one you've smoked today."

"I know. I don't smoke much."

"Then why now?"

He finally got the cigarette lit. "Because I want so damn bad to kiss you I don't know what to do."

"Kiss me then."

"No."

"Why?"

"Two reasons. One, you wouldn't like it, and two, it wouldn't help me much because then I'd just want to keep going."

"I don't want to be a tease, Allen. I always thought that was a mean thing to do."

"It is, and you're not. You haven't lied to me. I just—I just hope that one day you're going to feel the way I do right now, and I hope I'm the one there when you do."

"For your sake, I hope so too," Cheryl said.

"For both of our sakes. I'm okay. Here, I'm okay now. You want to snuggle back down and finish watching the movie?"

Already, in the hour and a half since intermission, he could feel a difference in her. Her tension was less, and it left faster. When the movie was over, she stayed curled against him for a moment before uncurling and returning to her side of the car.

·*Three*·

"*Now*," he said, passing the red exit sign, "I go back on duty. I have to go look at the Caddo Springs Post Office substation. Want me to drop you off at home? I don't have time to come in."

"Allen, I'm not sure it's safe for you to go out there alone in the middle of the night without even a two-way radio. Take me with you. I can sleep late tomorrow."

He glanced at her. "Okay," he said, "thanks. But there's no reason why it shouldn't be safe; I've been going out there every night for three weeks."

"What are we going to Caddo Springs for?" Cheryl asked sleepily, a few minutes later. "I mean, does this tie in with the forgeries, or is it something else altogether?"

"I'm not real sure," Allen answered. "To start with, we've been having some mail theft out of the Caddo Springs substation. It's not internal; there's just one postal employee there, and she's fifty-seven and has been there since she was twenty-one. But mail is going from inside the post office. Some of it's checks, and they're turning up forged, but there's been other mail going too. So I'm keeping an eye on what's there when, trying to set up a pattern. Some nights I sit out there all night, but there's just one of me. I can't do it all the time. So the rest of the time I spot-check. And to keep Miss Esther, who certainly isn't involved, from getting all in a tizzy, I do my spot-checking in the middle of the night."

"No, I wouldn't expect Miss Esther to be involved," Cheryl agreed. "But may I assume security is not her strong point?"

"You may. But she's not quite as scatty as she looks. She does generally remember to lock her desk, put negotiables and stamps in the safe, and lock the doors."

"Well, that's something," Cheryl said. "You just don't know how many times I've seen burglaries in which nobody had bothered to lock up the valuables, and everybody was furious at the police when the stuff went missing.''

"No, but I can make a good guess," Allen answered. "Lady, I've been in this business nineteen years." He fumbled in his pocket. "Damn! I wish I knew where my cigarette lighter went to."

"It's got to be in the car somewhere," Cheryl pointed out.

"Oh, yeah, I'll find it tomorrow," Allen agreed. "No big deal. I just hate to lose stuff in a rented car."

He pulled up in front of the little store. "And why anybody was talked into agreeing to put a substation into *that*," he commented, "I'll never know. It looks like a good breeze would blow it down."

"It's been there for eighty years," Cheryl answered, "and it's likely to be good for another eighty. And really, it's a very useful location. There are a lot of weekend and summer cabins on those little roads going down to the lake, and more people live there the year around than you might think."

"Not questioning the location," he agreed amiably. "Just the sturdiness of the building. I'll only be a minute. You don't mind waiting, do you? My key's to the back door, and there's no sense in both of us breaking our necks."

The store sat a little way back from the road in a bare red clay parking lot littered on the sides with scrap metal and wood overgrown with pokeberry and Queen Anne's lace and dotted in front with metal pop tops that sparkled in the headlights. "Harbison's Gro. and Mkt." said the sign between the two dull red gasoline pumps. "Cold Beer" announced another sign. Below that, in wavering black paint, someone had hand printed "Worms and Poles." Cheryl couldn't see the sign hanging from the eaves, but memory supplied it: U. S. Post Office Substation, Caddo Springs, Texas.

Looking at the dimly seen bulk of rubbish piled around all the exits, she answered, "No, I don't mind."

Halfway out of the car, he paused to glance back at her. "Look, about tonight, I'm sorry if I upset you."

"No reason to be sorry. It's not your fault. Go look at your—at whatever it is you're looking at." He could barely make out her face, but her voice said she was smiling at him.

"It's more *for* than *at*," he answered ruefully. "I wish to God I had something to look *at*. I still don't even know—" He paused, mentally shook himself. "Oh, well, you want to get home sometime tonight." He went on toward the darkened building, reaching in his pocket for the key, which he kept on a separate ring. He was walking wide, out in the parking lot away from the building, trying to avoid the broken glass in the weeds.

The key in his hand, he began whistling. Logic would probably dictate a flashlight, but he had good night vision and he didn't want to use a flashlight when part of the object of being here was to avoid spooking anybody who might be inside. With that thought in mind, he stopped whistling.

He was more nervous than he had admitted to Cheryl, not because of the night or the isolation, but because of the background of the case, a background he hadn't yet told anybody in Caddo County. He hadn't told anyone because he hadn't been sure, not until today, when he put together what John Arnold had told him with everything else. But now he was almost certain that this case was fitting into a pattern.

Theft of checks from mail boxes followed by forgery is common. And internal mail theft is not utterly uncommon. And very good forged identification, although not common, is not so rare as could be wished. But in the last two years this was the third time in the ArkLaTex in which all three elements had coincided. In the other two cases, postal inspectors had also been sent in—one the first time; two the second. The first time there was no known pattern to spot; the second, no pattern was spotted until too late.

But each time, the arrival of the postal inspector had signalled a flurry of other crimes. Once, it was a hijacked mail truck; both times, it had been post office robberies, all occurring within a single week, beginning about a month after the postal inspector's arrival. That alone meant that if this case was really the pattern, he could expect to have a somewhat hairy week coming up.

But that wasn't all.

In the second of those cases, the one in Louisiana, one of the inspectors assigned to the case had walked in on a post office robbery and been fatally shot by someone so thoroughly masked that it wasn't possible for witnesses to be certain even of the race, much less the sex, of the killer.

In both cases, not another thing had happened after the post office robbery, and none of the identifiable items from either robbery had ever surfaced.

This wasn't as safe a job as Allen had implied to Sergeant Hall. There had been postal inspectors a long time before there was an FBI or a Secret Service, and they didn't all die in their beds.

Well, Allen thought, the pattern's about clear now. I'll call Fort Worth tomorrow and see if the division inspector in charge has a team to send in. The investigation in Louisiana was still technically open and would be until the case was cleared, but the team had closed down and gone home, leaving only two men still following obscure leads. Maybe, he thought, maybe we can get him here, now, before he kills anybody else.

Funny, he couldn't recall it being quite that shadowy last night over against the wall—and then he realized he wasn't seeing shadows, he was seeing a car. Just as he realized that, the car began to move. In the moonlight, he saw a glint of something silver, and then he didn't know whether he actually heard the shot or not or whether the crack of the shot and the explosion of agony came so close together that sound and pain hit his brain together as one entity. He tried not to fall, but suddenly he was lying face down in the grass and brush, trying to get up on his side and trying not to cry out from the pain and knowing the second effort would have been quite as futile as the first, except that he didn't have the strength in him to do any more than breathe, and even that was difficult enough.

"Allen? Allen, don't try to move—"

That was Cheryl. He wanted to tell her that the idea of his moving was quite preposterous, only he forgot it before he could get his mouth open. Her hands were on him, turning him over, quickly checking the extent of injury. He heard her say under her breath, "Bleeding internal." Then she said, "Allen, I just tried the walkie-talkie, and it's gone out. I have to get in the building to call for an ambulance. Where are the door keys? Can you tell me where the keys are?"

Keys? At first he couldn't remember keys, but then he did. "Dropped them," he got out.

"Oh, *God!*" she said, "And no flashlight—I'll have to break in, then. Allen, hold on, I'll be back as fast as I can."

Dimly, he heard the sound of glass breaking. He guessed he must be drifting in and out of consciousness because it seemed just a moment later that Cheryl was back, sliding the jacket he'd left in the car under his head, saying, "There's an ambulance coming. How bad is it?"

"Bad," he tried to say. He got hold of her hand. Holding it tightly, he realized that he did not have the slightest idea of where he'd been hit. Then he slid on into darkness.

Cheryl was still sitting on the ground beside him, holding his now relaxed hand, when the ambulance arrived, moments before the police car. She jumped to her feet, waving the medics around the area where the white sedan had peeled out. "Be careful," she shouted, "this is a major crime scene, and we may have tire tracks."

"Okay," the EMT said, opening the ambulance door to pull the stretcher out. "They told us a shooting; how bad?"

"Vitals aren't too good," called the other EMT, already kneeling by Allen. "We might try to stabilize before we transport. Let's get an IV started. He's not bleeding much visibly, but there'll be some internal."

Allen's eyes flickered back open. "Am I going to die?" he asked steadily.

"No reason why you should," the EMT answered somewhat too cheerfully. "You're gonna be plenty sore tomorrow, though. Hey, didn't I just see you yesterday?"

"Yeah."

"Damn small world."

"Not—fair," Allen said from between gritted teeth. He started retching and tried to get up; both EMT's instantly grabbed him, one turning his head to one side so that he vomited mostly on the ground.

"Stay put," the one who had been cheerful told him. "I know it feels nasty to barf on your shoulder, but you can't get up now. We'll clean you off."

"Hurts—so—bad," he said and tried to draw his knees up. The EMT's let him do that. "Not very brave, am I?" he got out, able to speak more steadily with his knees up.

"Funny, I thought you were doing great," one EMT answered.

The other technician said, "Let's go on and transport."

"Yeah," the cheerful one agreed. "Cheryl, can you help us get him aboard? I need you to carry this IV bag. Hey, how'd you get out here before us? You don't usually."

"I was with him," she said. "We'd been to a movie." Her voice sounded wooden in her ears.

"Oh, lord, me and my big mouth," the EMT said.

Cheryl carried the IV bag with her right hand; with her left, she reached up and took Allen's left hand, carefully avoiding disturbing the tube in the top of it. Both his hands held tightly to hers and then released, but his eyes followed her as she climbed back off the ambulance. He lifted one hand briefly.

She watched as the ambulance left and then wiped her eyes with the back of her hand. He was right, she thought, it wasn't fair. It wasn't fair that he'd gotten shot twice in two days; that was what he had been going to say. But it wasn't fair, either, for the nicest man she'd ever met to be hurting like that, and it wasn't fair for her not to have kissed him—it wouldn't, she thought, have hurt me to kiss him tonight.

She turned and nearly bumped into Sergeant Kenneth Hall. "Excuse me," she muttered.

"What happened, Cheryl?" he asked. "Tell me from the start, everything you saw."

"What's the start?" she answered. "We got out here about one A.M."

When Allen got out, she told Hall, he left the car door open and went past the rear of the car, walking wide around the far side of the building to avoid the broken glass in the weeds.

Cheryl had turned off the radio and shifted in her seat so that she could watch him. Not that she was nervous—Cheryl was never nervous—but in the dark she liked to know what was going on.

And the old white sedan must have been parked on the far side of the store, toward the back, close to the wall and hugging the shadows. It shot out suddenly without its headlights on. Cheryl caught a glimpse of someone with bushy hair behind the steering wheel, sitting low. As the car went between her and Allen, she could barely see someone moving on the passenger side. Something glinted silver in the moonlight.

The shot hadn't quite finished echoing when the car squealed out onto the road, its lights coming on just too late for her to be able to read the license plate. Then it was gone and she could see Allen again.

He had been lying face down in the weeds, very still.

"Where was your gun?" Sergeant Hall asked.

"The same place as Allen's," she answered bitterly. "In the back seat. We weren't on duty. We'd been to a movie. We went to the drive-in. Do you wear a gun at the drive-in?"

"No, Cheryl, I don't wear a gun at the drive-in," Sergeant Hall answered resignedly. "And I'd like to say I'd put it back on if I was going from the drive-in to an isolated bait shop, but I don't really know that I would. All right, let's see those tire tracks you're so anxious to pre-serve.''

"How'd you know about them?"

"Because Rudy drove up right behind the ambulance. I'm quite aware that you haven't seen him yet."

She glanced around at Patrolman Rudy Garcia. "Hi," he said, "just guarding the crime scene. How is he, Cheryl?"

"I don't know," she said, "he was gut shot." She'd used the phrase before. It had never mattered to her before if somebody was gut shot or lung shot, because it had never been anyone who mattered to her. This department had never lost an officer.

"Are you going to be okay?" the sergeant asked. She realized she'd been staring at the blood on the ground. Not much blood; he hadn't bled much.

"I'm always okay at crime scenes," she said. That was true, of course; other people vomited at crime scenes, but Cheryl never had. And that was how this would have to be. Until she could get home for whatever was left of the night, she had to make herself believe that this was only a crime scene.

They could follow the path of the white sedan from the crushed dew-berry vines under the eaves, clear out to where it had peeled out getting onto the road. But this had been a dry May; there was not one inch of usable tire track.

They checked outside the store thoroughly, finding no sign of a break-in except for Cheryl's, which they patched with a sheet of plyboard. They'd have to replace the glass later. They found Allen's keys where he had dropped them and checked inside. There, too, there was no sign of a break-in; no post office boxes appeared to have been tampered with; without the ghost of an idea of what Allen had been watching, there was no way to check on it.

"I think we've done about all we can do here," Hall said.

"For now," Cheryl agreed. "We need to leave someone out here tonight, though, and come back again by daylight."

"I don't see that that's necessary," the sergeant answered. "I mean, look, he was shot from a moving car. There are no tire tracks. The bullet stayed in him. What else do you expect to find?"

"I just think—"

"It's not necessary," Sergeant Hall interrupted. "Now, would you mind telling me what you were doing wandering around at one o'clock in the morning with the postal inspector?''

"Who would you rather I was wandering around at one o'clock in the morning with?'' Cheryl demanded. "Anyhow, you told me to work with him this week.''

"Not at one A.M. I didn't.'' But then Hall shrugged. "*I* don't care,'' he added. "It's not my problem what you do at one A.M. or who you do it with. Look, kid, don't fret all night. He'll be okay.''

"Don't call me kid!'' The retort was automatic.

"Sorry, you're not a kid, you're a cop, and you were out here at one A.M. with the postal inspector because you were working, and the moon is made of green cheese. How do you want to get back into town? Want to ride with me?''

"I'll just sit out here on the—''

"Nobody is going to sit on this crime scene all night and that's final,'' Hall said. "There's no sense in it. Now, how do you want to get back into town?''

"I'll drive Allen's car. We can't just leave it out here all night, not if nobody's staying. And I want to go by the hospital and see—''

"They won't let you in,'' Hall interrupted.

"They will if I'm working it.'' In the moonlight, her eyes flashed a challenge.

"If you're—okay. Fine. You work it. But I don't think there'll be much working done because this county will be crawling with feds by morning, and they'll be working it themselves. But if you're going to work it from our end, go by the office and make a report. Hell, you've got to anyway, you're the only witness.'' He got in his car, slammed the door, gunned the engine, and left.

Cheryl looked at the rookie patrolman driving the one remaining uniform car, and said briskly, "Go on and go ten-eight. I don't need a backup to drive a car in.''

The rookie blushed, looked at the isolated store and then at Cheryl, and said, "Yeah, sure. Okay.'' The last thing visible as he turned left and headed back toward town was the lettering on his brown trunk lid, the white letters that read "Caddo County Police Department.''

Caddo County, Texas. A little county beside one shore of a big lake. The Caddo County Police Department had been in existence for only six years; it had been formed under a six-year-old agreement intended to increase efficiency when all the little city police forces had merged to create it. A still not always workable entity, it was housed, for want of anywhere else, in the basement of the new court house and was still barely accepted, much less welcomed, by old-timers.

Cheryl Burroughs, who had been in the Caddo County Police Department for two years as a secretary and four years as an officer, went now and got into the postal inspector's car. She didn't have to adjust the seat much; Allen was short. But as she leaned over to reach for the seat belt she caught sight of his cigarette lighter. So that was where he'd dropped it, two hours ago when they couldn't figure out where it had gone. And for a moment she gave in to some quite unofficial tears, before starting the car and following down the same road the ambulance had just taken.

At the police station, she got out just long enough to run in and dictate a report onto a cassette for Kathy to type the next day. Then, still in Allen's rented car, she drove to the emergency room parking lot.

"Hello," the head nurse said. "You're here about the shooting victim, of course?"

"Yes, how is he?"

"The doctor hasn't said yet. He's looking at X-rays right now. Do you need to see the victim?"

"How's he feeling?" One time, she'd had to go in and try to interview a shooting victim just after he'd arrived at the hospital because they thought he might die and they needed some answers. She hadn't gotten much information, but even years later she couldn't forget the inhuman sounds of his agony. She didn't want to see Allen like that; she didn't want Allen to have to remember, later, that she had seen him like that, with pain completely robbing him of his dignity.

"He's had some medication, and he's staying very calm. He may be able to talk to you. I know he wants to because he's asked for you a couple of times."

"Okay," she said, "which room?"

"He's in C."

Cheryl opened the door and went in quietly. "Allen?" she asked. His eyes opened and then widened. "Hi," he said weakly.

"Wasn't too good a backup this time, was I?"

"Uh-uh. Superman might've helped. But nobody else."

"I'm working it," she said. "I didn't think I could talk Sergeant Hall into letting me, but I did."

"Good," he said. His eyes closed for a minute and then reopened.

"But I don't know how much of the working you'll get to do. There'll be a bunch of people from my regional headquarters in Fort Worth and some FBI people by tomorrow. They don't consider federal agents too expendable. Have you got my car?"

"Yeah. And I found your cigarette lighter. I'll give it back to you when you get in a room."

"Can't smoke anyway. Oxygen and stuff." He moved cautiously. "It doesn't hurt so much now, as long as I stay still, only it feels so weird I can't stay still."

"Stay still anyway. Did you see anything, Allen?"

"I saw the car when it started moving, and I don't think there was two seconds from then 'til I was hit. I lost track of time after that, but the car must have been gone in another two seconds. I saw— something silver. It might've been a chrome gun, but I don't know. There were two people in the car, but I don't know what they looked like or what the car looked like. That's all. Cheryl?"

"Hmm?"

"This is going to fit in with my case. There's a lot more to it that I haven't told you because I wasn't sure yet, and I don't have time to tell you now."

"I oughtn't to be letting you talk anyway."

"Try and stop me." He stirred again. "I don't know how long it'll be before I can talk again, and I'll be mostly talking to federal agents for a while then. Cheryl, they're going to send in a team from Fort Worth, probably four or five guys. McCain will probably be in charge of it. That's Jim McCain. He's a real take-charge guy, not as laid back as most of us in this business are, and he and I don't always get along so good."

"Will he work with me?"

"He'll work with the department. I don't know about with you. I don't think you'll like him. Hall will."

"Allen, I want to catch this person myself."

"Just remember that he killed one man besides trying to kill me."

"That's why—killed what man?"

"Another postal inspector. That is, if this situation is what I think it is. And I don't want you to get into any trouble. Hey, did they leave somebody sitting out there?"

"No."

"Oh, shit. McCain's not going to like that one damn bit."

"Allen, can I Xerox your notes? In case McCain won't work with me?"

"Yes, but don't tell him you did. Turn my car in to the rental agency; that'll give you the excuse to have my briefcase, because you can't turn the car in until Monday. Drive it till then if you want to, unless McCain takes it away from you. But listen, when he asks for my briefcase, you've got to give it to him. And give him all my keys except my house and car key. And work with him as best as you can. He's got a tongue like a razor blade, but he's a real good investigator. And Cheryl?"

"Yeah?"

"If you're going to stay on this, be careful. Be damned careful. I couldn't stand for you to be going through what I am." He coughed and caught his breath sharply.

"Allen, please stop talking now."

"Be careful."

"I will. I promise. But please don't try to talk any more now."

"Okay," he said, "but hold my hand." His eyes drifted shut again.

Cheryl sat for a minute holding his hand and then, absentmindedly, she began running her fingers up and down his arm, just the way she'd pet a kitten.

He opened his eyes again. "I was thinking," he said, "that this might be a good time to stop smoking."

"I wish you would."

"Do you?" he asked. "Why?"

"I don't like the way it smells."

In a carefully casual voice, he asked, "Did Uncle Jack smoke?"

"Yes," Cheryl said.

"Please put the cigarette lighter in the trash can," he said. "I mean right now. I want to hear it drop."

"I can't. I didn't bring it in. And you are the oddest man I've ever met."

"How?"

"You're lying up there with a bullet in you and worrying about whether I like you to smoke?"

He breathed carefully for a couple of minutes and then said, "For a few minutes tonight I didn't think I was going to have any rest of my life left. And when I decided I was, after all, I felt like I ought to think about what was important in that rest of my life I nearly lost. And cigarettes aren't. That's all. And I wish if you were going to pretend that my arm is a puppy dog you'd notice which way the hair grows."

"I'm sorry."

"I don't mind being a puppy dog; it's just that my hair doesn't grow that way. Cheryl? If I die tonight, remember that I would have been in love with you if we'd had just a little more time."

"You're not going to die," Cheryl answered, startled.

"I know," Allen answered. "But just in case."

"Okay," Cheryl answered, feeling very awkward and not at all sure of what to say.

A nurse entered, followed by Sergeant Hall. "Cheryl, I have to ask you to leave now because we've got to start getting him ready for surgery. Your sergeant said he'd take over in here."

"Oh, am I under guard?" Allen asked with great interest.

"No," Hall said, "but sometimes people remember things just as they're going under an anesthetic that they can't remember later."

"And they don't want me in here," Cheryl said, "because they're afraid I might see something." She stood up. "See you tomorrow."

"Do you have to cut off all my clothes?" Allen demanded a moment later.

"You wouldn't want them back anyway," the nurse replied cheerfully. Allen was beginning to be very tired of people being excessively cheerful at him. "The sergeant here will take care of whatever you've got in your pockets."

"The stuff in my pockets, give it to Cheryl," he said. "I already told her what to do with it."

"We'll do that, then," the nurse said and left again, presumably in search of something forgotten.

Allen closed his eyes. "I think that shot is finally starting to do something. I'm so dizzy I can't see straight. Ken?"

"Yeah?" The sergeant mentally blinked. He hadn't even been sure Allen knew his first name.

"Don't blame Cheryl. If she'd had a gun in her hand she couldn't have kept it from happening."

"I don't blame her."

"Good. She's a real good cop. And she's smart. I like her. I like her." His breathing was steady and even for about a minute, and then he added in a slurred voice, "I like her a lot."

When the nurse returned he was asleep, breathing slowly, his face finally relaxed. The nurse pulled up the side rails on the gurney. "He's not going to say anything else tonight," she told the sergeant.

In the hall, Cheryl was talking with Dr. Boyd. As Sergeant Hall emerged from the small room, the doctor was saying, "He should be all right, but Cheryl, you've got to get it through your head that this is going to take a while. If we don't get everything completely cleaned up and repaired, the man could end up with peritonitis. For that matter, he could anyway, but the more careful we are the less likely that is to happen."

"You take as long as it takes," Cheryl said. "That's not what I meant. All I meant was, it's Friday night—"

"It's Saturday morning," the surgeon interposed wearily.

"All right, it's Saturday morning, but I haven't been to bed yet. What I meant was, I don't want to have to wait till pathology opens Monday morning at nine o'clock to get that slug. I want to know now what kind of gun we're looking for."

"Cheryl," the sergeant said, "I don't see what difference it makes. You'll have to wait till Monday to take it to Garland anyway."

"Why Garland?" Dr. Boyd asked. "Why, for crying out loud, do you want to take this bullet to the other side of Dallas?"

"Because that's the closest crime lab," Cheryl said. "And I'll bet if I call Bill and tell him how serious this is, he'll meet me there tomorrow. Today. Saturday."

"Bill being the firearms examiner," Sergeant Hall explained to the doctor. "He might at that."

"I'll tell you what I can do," Dr. Boyd said. "Just as soon as I get to the bullet I'll have the circulating nurse bring it out to you, okay? But," he added as she started to speak, "you may be sitting here for a while. Because I am not going to butcher that man to get to the bullet. It's going to take as long as it takes. Is that clear?"

"Perfectly clear," Cheryl said.

"Doctor Boyd," the sergeant said.

"What is it now?"

"This is not just a case to her. She'd been on a date with the man; she was there when he was shot. And in case you don't know Cheryl very well, I'll add that to my definite knowledge this is the first date she's been willing to have in five years."

"It wasn't a—" Cheryl started to say. But then she said, "Well, I guess it was, sort of."

"Oh," the doctor said. "Cheryl, excuse the temper in that case. I misunderstood. I thought you were just being an eager beaver because you'd never had charge of working a shooting before."

"Then don't go on misunderstanding," Cheryl answered. "You better believe I'm an eager beaver. I want to know who shot Allen. Only the fact that I know I can't just go around shooting people keeps me from adding that I would like to have whoever tried to kill Allen in my gunsights. Please go take care of Allen now. Where do you want me to wait for that slug?"

"Third floor waiting room, east end. There's a couch up there. You might as well try to get some sleep. I figure it's going to take me at least an hour to get to the bullet."

She didn't think she could sleep. And at first she couldn't; every time she closed her eyes she saw Allen lying face down in the weeds, struggling to turn over on his side; Allen vomiting, drawing his knees up from the pain; Allen's face, pale and sweaty from shock but trying to smile, telling her he would quit smoking because he didn't want to smell like Uncle Jack.

Uncle Jack's been dead thirteen years, she thought. I don't even remember what he looked like. But then she did remember, saw his face as clearly as if he were there, so clearly she almost screamed; but she knew he was dead. He couldn't really be there, and anyhow she wasn't little Cheryl now. She had a gun, she could fight back.

Why should Allen pay for what Uncle Jack did?

And why should *I* pay for what Uncle Jack did?

And Holly's father. His name is Terry. Holly's with him because the judge said Terry can have Holly one month every summer. And I'm scared when Holly's with him, scared he might do her like Uncle Jack did me. Only she's just five, men don't—

Some men do.

Uncle Jack did.

Funny I never noticed before, Terry's eyes looked just like Uncle Jack's eyes. And Uncle Jack smoked Camels—and Terry smokes Camels.

Allen smoked Kools, but he's going to quit smoking now.

Allen, she thought. When Allen was smoking that last cigarette in the car after he lost his lighter, he wanted the same thing Terry and Uncle Jack wanted. But *they* looked just the same when they wanted it; Allen didn't. His eyes looked different. Their eyes glittered, like there was a fire behind them. Allen's eyes glowed like a fire too, but theirs had been forest fires and his was a hearth fire, warm and controlled and welcome.

Allen's eyes—Allen's hands—Allen's face.

"Cheryl?"

"Hmm? Oh! I didn't know I was asleep. What time is it, Yvonne?" She sat up. "Were you circulating nurse tonight?"

"Yes. And it's nearly four. You've slept about two hours."

"How's Allen?"

"The patient?"

"Yeah, the patient. That's Allen. How is he?"

"He was cut up some inside; that's why it's taking so long. Dr. Boyd said it looked like the bullet might have ricocheted off a rib and kind of bounced around some. But he's going to be fine."

"You're sure? He's really going to be all right?"

"Honest, he'll recover real fast. Say, you really care about him, don't you?"

"Yeah, I guess I do," Cheryl said. She wasn't really sure she was quite awake yet, talking with a nurse she'd known all her life at four A.M. in a hospital waiting room outside an operating room where a doctor was repairing Allen's insides like she'd mend one of Holly's torn dresses.

"I've got to get back in," Yvonne said, "but Dr. Boyd said for me to bring you this."

"Yeah. I was waiting for it." The slug, which Dr. Boyd persisted in calling a bullet, was sealed in a small clear plastic bottle, carefully wrapped in gauze squares and predictably labelled "Bullet removed from intestinal cavity of Allen Conyers" with the date and Yvonne's initials.

"How come? Will it tell you what kind of gun he was shot with?"

Cheryl opened the bottle and looked inside the gauze. "I can tell that right now," she said. "It was a .32. But when Bill looks at it, he'll be able to tell what brand of .32, and one of these days it'll tell somebody exactly which .32."

"But you have to find the gun to do that, don't you?"

"Sure, we have to find it, but it'll help to know what we're looking for."

Four A.M. Not much use to go home. But she needed a few more hours of sleep. She put the jar in her pocket so that she couldn't drop it, and lay back down on the couch. Instantly she was asleep, but with no dreams this time.

Yvonne woke her again at six. "Cheryl? He's in recovery. We don't usually let people in except family, but Dr. Boyd said we're real short-handed right now, and it would help if you could go sit with him for a while. He probably won't be waking up for about an hour yet, and I should be back by then. I'm doubling over this shift."

Allen's face was quite peaceful now, but still pale. An IV bottle was beside him, the tube going into the top of his left hand as it had been doing, Cheryl guessed, for five hours now. "You'll need to change that when he starts to wake up," she said. "He's left-handed."

"Oh, is he? Thanks, I'll do it right now. We didn't guess that because so many left-handed people wear their watches on the right, and we could tell he'd been wearing his on the left."

Allen stirred when the nurse put the new needle into his right hand; he said a name, but it wasn't Cheryl's name. "Lisa?" he said. "No, Lisa, please—don't—don't—" He shook his head from side to side. "Don't, please, Lisa."

The nurse leaned over him. "It's all right, she won't," she said soothingly. She looked at Cheryl and shrugged. "Whatever it is," she whispered. "He doesn't know what he's saying right now. Call me if he gets any more restless."

Allen shook his head. "She—already—did. I don't know why . . . I don't know why . . . Cheryl had *her* baby, but—but—Lisa—killed my baby."

So that's what's been eating him, Cheryl thought, and took his hands in hers. "Allen, listen to me."

Yvonne, nearly to the door, paused. "Cheryl, he's not hearing you. It's like he's having a nightmare."

Ignoring her, Cheryl repeated, "Allen, I'm here, Allen."

"Cheryl," he said, and the tension began to leave his face. But his eyes were still closed; it was as if he were trying to carry on a conversation in his sleep. "Cheryl?" he said again. "Lisa killed my baby. You have a baby. I don't have a baby. But you didn't want to tell me about your baby. Why?"

"I'll tell you about my baby now," Cheryl said. "Want me to?"

"Uh-huh. Holly. Her name's Holly. I saw a picture of her. Holly. That's like Christmas."

"That's because she was born in December. If you'll be quiet, I'll tell you about Holly."

"Uh-huh. Tell me about Holly."

"But you have to be quiet and still." She talked about Holly, talked as softly as if she were talking to Holly and Holly had been having a nightmare, talked for an hour, talked herself nearly hoarse, until Allen's eyes flickered open. "Hi," he said weakly.

"Hi, Allen."

"Were you talking to me, or did I dream that?"

"I was talking to you. How do you feel?"

He blinked. "Pretty rocky. Did I say anything when I was waking up?"

"Nothing much."

"Which means I said something."

"You said Lisa killed your baby. You said it twice. First you were begging her not to, and then you said she did it. Was Lisa your wife?"

"Yes. And she didn't actually kill a baby, what she did was have an abortion."

"If she didn't kill a baby, how do you define abortion?" Cheryl asked. "Okay, I know, skip it, it's a surgical procedure and a perfectly legal one at that."

Allen closed his eyes, and Cheryl suddenly realized he was crying, completely silently. "Allen, are you okay? Should I get the nurse?"

"I'm okay. I don't often do this now; it's just that I'm weak right now. Let me go on and get it said, because this may be the only time I'll be able to. Lisa just didn't want to be bothered, and she said she had a right not to be. I said I could understand that maybe, if she was sick, or if nobody else wanted the baby either, but she's never been sick a day in her life. I told her that if she'd just consent to be—inconvenienced—six more months, I'd find a way to take care of the child so that she wouldn't have to be bothered. But she didn't figure she could be bothered six more months. I tried to understand. I did try to understand, Cheryl. But I wanted that baby so much. And to her it wasn't a baby at all."

He was silent for a moment, not trying to wipe away or hide the tears. "That didn't leave much communication between us. So, after the divorce, I asked to be transferred out of New York City. We'd lived there seven years, but right then I didn't feel like even New York was big enough for Lisa and me both. I wanted a little office, the kind of place where one man is working everything. Most of them have been closed up, though, and the head shed said they wouldn't let me work alone right then anyway. But they got me out of New York—sent me to Miami for a couple of years and then to Dallas. By the time the slot here came up they'd decided I wasn't going to do anything stupid—they were worried about that at first, I think, because I was so shook up—and they let me come here."

"Is that what you wouldn't tell me?"

"Yes. Because I didn't figure I could get it out without crying. Cheryl, if Holly was five in December—that's when Lisa's baby would have been born—it would have been five in December, too. You had a lot more reason than she did. Why didn't you—?"

"I don't think I ever thought about it," Cheryl said. "I mean, I couldn't blame the baby for the situation even when it was just sort of a hypothetical baby. And it's horrible to think about that now because we're talking about Holly, and Holly's a person." She stood up. "Allen, I have to go take some stuff to the crime lab in Garland. Will you be okay if I leave you now?"

"Be fine," he said. "Cheryl, thank you for everything you've done. Have you realized yet that if you hadn't insisted on going with me I'd still be lying out there on the ground?"

"That's something else I don't want to think about," she answered. "I'll see you this evening. Or whenever."

"Cheryl?" The nurse stuck her head in the door. "Does he seem like he's about to wake up? There's a man out here named McCain who says he's absolutely got to talk to him as soon as he does, and the doctor okayed it."

Allen squinted his eyes tightly shut. "I am *not* sure I am up to seeing Jim McCain," he said. "But all right, let him come in."

"Wow, you did wake up fast," Yvonne said. "I'll get him."

Jim McCain was taller than Allen Conyers, younger than Allen Conyers, broader across the shoulders than Allen Conyers, and apparently somewhat more angry about the shooting than Allen was. His wiry ginger moustache was virtually bristling with indignation. He allowed Allen to introduce Cheryl to him, and then demanded, "What happened?"

"Cheryl knows," Allen said, "let her tell you."

"I'm going to talk with Cheryl later. Right now I want you to talk to me."

In ten sentences, Allen described the shooting. Then he said, "Jim, I got four hours of sleep night before last. I was still up running around at one A.M. last night, at which time I got shot. I stayed mostly conscious and hurting worse than you can imagine until after two. I've been in surgery, or just out of surgery, since then. Please, can you go do something else and come back and talk to me this afternoon? I've got to get some rest. All I can tell you now is that I don't know who shot me. I wish I did know."

It would have been inhuman to refuse. "Okay," McCain said. "Tell me where your notes are; maybe I can work from them some. Right now I'll go talk to—Cheryl, is that her name?" He looked around. Cheryl was gone.

Cheryl was downstairs on a pay phone in the lobby talking to a firearms examiner who had rapidly become much less sleepy and much less annoyed at an early Saturday morning telephone call than he had been one minute earlier. He had a question now, though. "Don't you think the FBI might want the slug to go to their lab? This is going to be a federal case, you know."

"But we have joint jurisdiction at least," she argued, "because it didn't happen on federal property. Oh, Bill, you know how long those big national labs take. I want to know what kind of gun now, not next September."

"They might not take so long on this sort of case," Bill said. "But look, I don't have to keep the slug. It shouldn't take me more than about fifteen minutes or so. How soon can you be here?"

"It's seven now," she said. "How about if I meet you there at ten-thirty?"

"I hope you've got a siren," he said dubiously. "That's a long way for three and a half hours. Okay, ten-thirty. Oh, since you're coming up anyway, how about bringing that other case?"

"That which other case?"

"That slug from your Ten Most Wanted and test firings from whatever guns are involved. Hall called me yesterday and said they were ready to come up, and I wouldn't mind checking them today too."

"Why such a hurry?" Cheryl asked.

"I just hope it was you," Bill said. "I think it would be fun. I could go around saying *I* know the woman who shot—"

"Oh, good grief," Cheryl said. "I'll see you at ten-thirty."

·Four·

Jim McCain was a very angry man.

There are approximately 1,800 postal inspectors in the United States. The student body of a moderately sized high school may be larger than that group. There is far too much work for them ever to get it all done. And some sorry, no-good punk somewhere in that back corner of America called the ArkLaTex had killed one, and now someone, possibly the same someone (judging from what little Allen had said), had put another out of action for a while. The killing had tied up six inspectors for two months; now five were gathered here. Which left proportionally fewer people to do the work that was far too great to be done at all.

Furthermore, Steve Karney had turned up from the FBI because the FBI shared jurisdiction on this, and Jim didn't particularly like to work with the FBI; they always, he thought, seem to think they're superior to everybody else.

Furthermore, he had managed to get only three hours of sleep the night before, and that was in a car somebody else was driving over a rough road.

And on top of everything else, he'd just asked who was guarding the crime scene. "Nobody," Sergeant Hall had answered incautiously.

"You mean nobody even cared enough to protect the scene?" McCain demanded.

"Now look," Hall objected, "we searched it last night and got all there was. There just wasn't anything."

"There wasn't—oh, uh-huh, I see. Did you get any pictures?"

"Of what?" Hall asked. "There wasn't anything to take a picture of."

"Then will you please," McCain said, "be good enough to direct or escort me to this unguarded crime scene so that I can look at what you didn't see and get some pictures of what you didn't find? And could you kindly lend me a couple of patrolmen to belatedly protect the area from any more neglect until I get a lab crew in, or shall I call a couple of my men off what I've already put them on and have them do that? Oh, and has anybody been able to locate Conyers's car? I need his notes, and he says they're in it.''

"His car's in the shop," Hall answered, glad they'd reached a question he could answer. "It was getting a new windshield.''

"Right. It was getting a new windshield because the old one got shot out," McCain agreed. "And this intrepid damn fool, having the day before yesterday successfully shot it out with one of the Ten Most Wanted, yesterday went out, *in* a rented car, *with* a girl, and got himself damn near blowed away by some local hood. Now, it is the whereabouts of this rented car about which I am inquiring.''

"I know where that is," Lloyd Methvin volunteered. "Cheryl decided to drive it to the lab because 16's air conditioning is still out. She said Allen told her she could.''

"Cheryl—took—it—to—*what* lab?" McCain demanded from between nearly clenched teeth.

"The crime lab in Garland. She called Bill and then took off up there about an hour ago. I know, because she came by here to get those test slugs from Thursday to take along. She was going anyway, with Allen's slug.''

"*She did what?*" McCain shouted. "Oh, my God, I don't believe it! You don't protect the crime scene, you don't know where his car, with all his notes in it, is until somebody tells you, you assign the case—a serious assault on a federal officer—to some damn little meter maid and then she runs off somewhere with—''

"Now hold on!" Hall shouted back. "That's about enough! I won't defend my not protecting the crime scene; I should have, and Cheryl tried to talk me into it. But Cheryl is not, and never was, a meter maid. She's been a detective for two years, and the only reason she hasn't worked killings before is because we don't have many around here. I assigned her the case because she'd already been working with Allen and knows the background, and because she cares. If anybody can find out who shot him she can, and I'll bet she can find out faster than you damn feds, who don't know the territory and don't care to learn it. And in case you didn't understand Lloyd, Cheryl took the slug to our state firearms examiner so that we'll know what kind of firearm we're looking for—or maybe you'd rather look at all the guns in Caddo County, and Harrison County, and Cass County, and Gregg County, and Morris County, and Marion—" He wound down, somewhat out of breath.

"Okay, okay," McCain said, "I take it back. Excuse me. Forget what I said. The problem is that we've got a lab truck of our own en route from our regional lab in Memphis, and we'd kind of figured on letting them do all the lab work. And I'm sure Cheryl is Dick Tracy's smarter sister, only I never tried to work with a woman on this serious a case before. Okay? Can we get along now?" He looked around, spotted the coffee pot, and headed for it. "I'm sorry," he added, "I'm about out on my feet. Whether you know it or not, what we now figure is very probably the same bastard killed another postal inspector, a young fellow by the name of Matt Elton, eight months ago in Bossier City. We drove here not knowing whether we were going to find Allen alive or dead; all we knew was that your dispatcher called my boss and said the postal inspector in Lakeport was gut shot and on the way to the hospital."

"We didn't know then what kind of shape he was in, and we figured you'd rather know about the shooting immediately than wait till we found out his condition," Hall said. "And there's one more thing you'd better know."

"What's that?" McCain asked, sitting down with the cup of coffee in front of him.

"Best as I can tell," Hall told him, "Cheryl is just on the verge of being in love with Allen Conyers. And if I was to have my bet, I'd bet he's even more so with her."

"And you're letting her work the shooting? Can you trust her judgment on it if she's that emotionally involved?"

"He trusted her last night," Hall answered. "And he'd likely be dead now if he hadn't."

"Okay," McCain said. "Can you get me a couple of patrolmen to guard the crime scene? And I need about 250 yards of rope and some pylons like the ones used to mark a track for footracing."

"Lloyd, round up Coach Mosier and see if he can loan you the rope and pylons," Hall said. He picked up the phone and called dispatch. "See if you can find me a couple of patrolmen who want some overtime, and have them meet me at Harbison's to guard a crime scene." He put the phone down. "Now, you want to go on out there, right?"

"Right," McCain said.

The front door to the post office was open, but the door leading into the back was securely padlocked, and the outside back door was both deadbolted and padlocked. There were only three cars at Harbison's, and all three were on the bait shop side. It did not appear there had been much, if any, traffic around the post office.

"The best we can determine from what Cheryl said last night," Hall told McCain, "is that the suspect vehicle was parked right here with its lights off. There aren't any street lights here, of course, and with the moonlight coming from over that way, well, they just couldn't see the car until it moved. Cheryl was sitting on the passenger side of Allen's car; it was parked up here."

"Wait a minute," McCain said. "I didn't realize, from what was said before I got here, just how isolated this place is. Who called the ambulance?"

"Cheryl, of course. They had a walkie-talkie with them, but its batteries had gone out, and Allen dropped the door keys when he fell. We found them later, right here. You can see where this pile of rocks marks—"

"Hold on. Is this where he fell?" McCain was looking at the drying puddle of blood on the clay.

"Yeah."

"He didn't bleed much."

"It was mostly internal," Hall said.

"Okay, so Cheryl found the keys," McCain said, "and then—?"

"No, I found the keys later. Cheryl had to break in to get to a telephone. She didn't figure she had time to hunt for the keys then."

"Where'd she break in?"

"This front window. We covered it back up."

McCain looked at the window, set high in the wall. From the one glimpse he'd had of Cheryl, he remembered her as being rather short. He wondered how she'd gotten up to the window. He wondered how he'd get to it if he were trying to get into it in the middle of the night, in the dark, with a wounded man in critical need of an ambulance lying outside. I'd climb up on that railing, he thought, and looked at the railing. There were fresh scuff marks on it. She'd climbed it. Resourceful, he thought. Apparently not as brainless as he'd thought from looking at her.

Lloyd Methvin drove into the parking lot, pylons and rope in his trunk, the trunk lid partially closed over them and semi-fastened with a length of the rope. He drove in rather fast, spraying gravel, and Mc-Cain mentally winced. "Where do we want these pylons?" he asked.

"Right here," McCain said.

They roped off the side of the parking lot clear out to the edge of the road. Then McCain got large cardboard signs out of the trunk of his car and stapled them to the rope. The area was now clearly marked, "CRIME SCENE! KEEP OUT!"

The walkie-talkie in its pouch on Sergeant Hall's belt had been busy with traffic stops and other routine matters. Now it said, "Headquarters to car 5?"

Hall took it out of its pouch. "Five, go ahead."

"Sergeant, there's some guys here from Memphis saying they're supposed to go to a crime scene. Know anything about it?"

"Ten-four; who's getting the overtime?"

"Garcia and Squirrel Riley."

"Have they left the PD yet?"

"Let me check." In a minute he said, "That's negative. They're both in the locker room."

"Ten-four. Have them lead the crew from Memphis out to Harbison's. Tell them to twenty-nine me and McCain out here."

"You and who?"

"McCain. The fellow they're supposed to meet. We're already on the scene."

"Ten-four."

"Talk to me about Garcia and Squirrel Riley," McCain said. "This lab crew's been driving all night. They'll do some work here and then they may want to leave and get a little rest and come back. Can these two be trusted to really protect the area, or will they smoke and look around to see what they can find and that sort of thing?"

"Garcia's good," Hall said, "and he won't let Riley get into too much trouble."

"You need to let them both know their asses will be mud if they do get into trouble," McCain said. "Look, I'm not trying to pick another fight; I shouldn't have to start with, and I'm just asking for information. But I really do want to know why you didn't leave anybody out here last night."

"You've seen it for yourself," Hall said. "There's no tire tracks. There's no footprints. There's no shell casings. The slug rode away still in Allen's belly. There's no sense collecting blood samples; we know it's Allen's blood because he was lying in it when we got here. I honestly don't know what else you expect to find."

McCain looked around silently. "From your point of view, nothing," he said finally. "We won't find anything at all that will lead us to anybody or anything. But we're proceeding on the assumption that we'll develop a suspect in other ways, and then anything that can help nail that suspect will help. Now, there was a car parked over there in that clump of vines and brush. It probably carried away some of that vegetation in its undercarriage. If we can find it soon enough, that vegetation will still be there."

He walked over toward where the car had been parked, continuing, "It might have dripped some transmission fluid, or some oil, or some air conditioner fluid, and laboratory analysis can tell us not necessarily that it *is* the same car, but that it *could be* the same car. There's sand and clay and gravel in the parking lot. Some of that may be lodged in the grooves of the tires, and if the suspect got out and walked around any while he was waiting, there might be some on his shoes or inside the car where it fell off his shoes. And the car may have scraped up against the side of the building; if it did, there'll be paint transfer. And so on, and so on. The lab crew'll work a grid pattern. They'll cover every square inch of the ground, and they'll find everything there is to find."

Hall surveyed the now roped-off scene. "I know all that," he said finally. "I've been taught it in schools. But we don't have the facilities, and I guess I'd sort of forgotten that anybody else really did either."

"I shouldn't have hollered at you about it," McCain said. "I should have told your dispatcher last night that we'd have a lab crew coming down."

"Headquarters to car 5?"

"Five; go ahead."

"Can you twenty-eight the station?"

"Ten-four." He turned to McCain. " 'Scuse me, I've got to make a telephone call."

"I've got Cheryl on another line," the dispatcher said. "Let me patch her through to you."

As usual with a conference call, the transmission was a little faint. Cheryl said, "I'm in Garland, can you hear me?"

"Yeah, Cheryl, but not very well. Has Bill—"

"He looked at the slugs," Cheryl interrupted. "He says Allen was shot with something called a .32 Omega. It's got ten lands and grooves and a right-hand twist."

"Just a minute," Hall said. "Hey, McCain."

"Yeah?"

"Cheryl says he was shot with a .32 Omega."

"Give me the phone."

"Okay. Cheryl, McCain wants to speak to you."

"Are you still at the lab?" McCain demanded.

"Yes, I am."

"Absolutely, positively, without fail, bring that slug back with you. It's got to be compared with another slug also fired from a .32 Omega."

"I was going to anyway," Cheryl said. "Let me speak to Sergeant Hall again." McCain returned the phone, and Cheryl said, "He just got through comparing the slugs from Thursday. You know those test firings Allen and I did?"

"Yeah, I know those test firings. What about them?"

"Well, we both hit Pitts in the chest. But the slug the medical examiner said actually killed him came out of my gun."

"So hooray for you," Hall said. "You feel okay about it?"

"Sure," Cheryl said. "We sort of had to."

"That you did. Get you something to eat before you head back."

"Will do."

Hall turned back to speak to McCain, but McCain wasn't there. He'd walked back out to the road, where what looked like a large white bread delivery truck with a ladder on its roof had pulled up. The lab truck, Hall guessed and was vaguely surprised to see that it was unmarked. He didn't approach the truck; he hoped the technicians would be through with whatever they had to say about the unguarded crime scene before he had to meet them.

McCain headed back toward him, followed by the two men who had clambered out of the truck. "These are Buck Oliver and Danny Carr," he said, without the least indication which was which. "They've got it now. You want to instruct your men? Then let's head on in. It's—" He looked at his watch. "It's nearly eleven. We should be able to talk to Conyers now. Can your dispatcher get Karney to meet us at the hospital? There's no sense in Conyers having to go through the story once for us and once for the Bureau."

"I don't see why you and the FBI are both working on it to start with," Hall commented.

"It's because technically an assault on a federal officer is an offense handled by the FBI," McCain answered. "But we're certainly not going to sit and do nothing when it's one of our people. Plus it's certainly tied up with the cases he is working on, which *are* our jurisdiction. Actually, it's a lot like you assigning Cheryl to it when you know good and well your county is going to be full of federal officers."

"I see that," Hall said. "We all want to clear it."

"So we all want to work with, and not against, each other," McCain went on. "Because it's not important who clears it, it's just important that it gets cleared."

Hall looked at him sideways. "Do you really believe that?"

McCain looked startled and then, for the first time since Hall had met him, grinned. "Hell, no," he answered. "Cheryl wants to clear it, you want to clear it, I want to clear it, I haven't met Karney yet but I figure—"

"I know Karney," Hall said drily. "He wants to clear it himself." McCain glanced over curiously, and Hall added, "Karney—uh—is very young. He still has a case of rookie-itis."

"Oh," McCain said.

"But I hope it's somebody else instead of him," Hall added.

"How so?"

"Well," Hall said, "it's like this. I've noticed that when me and the postal inspector work on something, the headline says 'local police' do whatever it is. And when me and the Secret Service work on something, the headline says 'local police and Secret Service.' And when me and the FBI do something, the headline says 'FBI clears case' and if the Caddo County Police get mentioned at all it's where the story continues on page 19. And me, I'm just conceited enough to like to get a little of the credit for my organization."

This time McCain laughed. "Well, I feel that way, too," he admitted. "Up to now, the Postal Inspection Service has dodged publicity, but that policy has changed. We'll still try to make sure you get your share of the credit, but we've got to start getting our share, too."

"How come?"

"Policy shift. Nobody told me, but my guess is that our lack of publicity has hurt our funding."

"Makes sense. Look," Hall said, "why don't you let me just drop you by the hospital and pick you up later instead of going with you? I've got other work to do, and I feel pretty sure Cheryl can get all the information we need from Allen."

"No problem. As soon as Cheryl gets back with that rented car, I'm going to take it over anyway."

"What was that you were saying about another slug?" Hall asked.

"The pattern I told you about on the way out here," McCain said. "It first showed up in Arkansas. Of course, it wasn't a pattern, really, until it showed up the second time, in Louisiana."

"Yeah. You said Allen had just spotted it here," Hall said. "But you didn't say anything about a killing."

"There wasn't one in Arkansas. But there was in Louisiana. I know I mentioned it in your office." McCain's breathing was rather obviously carefully controlled as he continued. "A young inspector, fresh out of training. Matt Elton. Talk about a case of rookie-itis, he had one, too. You and me, we walk in on a robbery going down, we back off until the robbers have cleared the public building. Not Matt. He tried to draw down on them."

"You knew him?"

"I knew him. He lived about nineteen hours. He—uh—didn't like those nineteen hours much."

"Conscious some, then?"

"Yeah. He talked to us. But he didn't know anything."

"No more than Allen does?"

"Less. I told you, he was a kid. He didn't even know what to look for."

They went on to the hospital in silence. "Call me to come by for you," Hall said. "Or if Cheryl's back by then, I'll send her on over."

Cheryl was beginning to yawn as she drove into the west end of Caddo County at two-fifteen. But she turned on the walkie-talkie she'd picked up that morning and said into it, "Car 17 is back inside the county."

"Ten-four, car 17."

She didn't feel any particular emotion about now knowing for sure that she was the one who had killed Jimmie Pitts. She wondered whether she should feel some emotion, whether she was somehow repressing it for it to would creep back at a later date. But maybe, she thought, maybe she just didn't have time to care.

It was easier not to care. It was easier to just be a cop.

She yawned again and thought, briefly, about pulling over to the side of the road to sleep in the car. But the car would be too hot once the air conditioner was turned off.

The radio came alive. "Do I have a detective unit around the west end of the county?" Judging from the ensuing silence, he apparently did not have a detective unit around the west end of the county. "Car 17, what is your location?"

"I'm about half a mile from Carter's Grocery," she answered, "but I'm off duty and not even in a county car."

"Well, I got to have a detective at the boat ramp at Marsh's Landing. We got a report of a DB in the lake."

And a conscientious detective cannot go home and go to bed leaving a corpse floating in Caddo Lake no matter how tired she might be. "Ten-four," Cheryl said resignedly, "be en route." She made a U-turn in the middle of the road.

There were two cars and a pickup truck with a boat trailer tied behind it parked at Marsh's Landing. With some dismay, Cheryl recognized the pickup. It belonged to Waymon Thomas, her sister's new boyfriend. All we need, she thought, is for a reporter to find a body, or, good lord, what if Charlotte found it?

Charlotte might not have found it, but she'd apparently looked. She had rather obviously been being sick. "It's awful, Cheryl," she choked.

"I'm sure it is," Cheryl agreed and walked on down the ramp to where Waymon was happily taking pictures. She wondered why; not even the most obnoxious scandal sheet could possibly print those scenes. "I need all of you to go on up on the bank now," she said, her identification displayed in her hand.

An avidly staring grey-haired man said from around his chewing tobacco, "Buzz off, lady, we're waiting for the cops." He spat tobacco juice.

"I *am* the cops," she replied, "and I don't need you spitting on the crime scene. Wait up there on the bank; we'll need to talk to everybody." After a moment, she added, "Waymon, that means you too."

"Power of the press?"

"Power of the press's ass, you know you don't go trampling down a crime scene."

"But I found it," he protested.

"And then you let Charlotte see it, and she's been puking. Up on the bank, Waymon, now."

"All right," he said disgustedly and went.

It wasn't a DB. It was two DB's. Lucille Brantley was on her back, sightless eyes up to the sky, wedged in some rocks and cypress knees to the right of the ramp. Her feet were tied with red nylon rope. Her hands weren't visible; judging from the position of her shoulders, Cheryl felt fairly sure the hands, too, would prove to be tied behind her back. Her mouth was open; she'd been screaming when she died. Someone had used a knife on her. She'd been stabbed, finally, but what had happened before she was stabbed wasn't pretty.

Her head was out of the water. There was a piece of cardboard stuck in her mouth, and by leaning forward, Cheryl could see that it was a business card printed in dark blue. Centered on the top third of the card was a shield; across the eagle's wings that formed the top of the shield was a blue bar. Across it in white letters was the word Inspector. The rest of the shield contained a round-cornered square with a small eagle bounded by the words "United States Postal Service." Centered below the shield were two lines. "A. D. Conyers" was the first, and the second read "Postal Inspector." Below that was his office telephone number and his mailing address, and he'd inked in his home telephone number.

The card Allen had given Lucille in the laundromat. The card she didn't want, the card she had thrown on the floor. Apparently, she had picked it up later.

Why had she been killed, Cheryl wondered. Was it because they thought she'd talked or because they were afraid she would? Or was it just as an example to the other women, a warning to keep their mouths shut, to stay away from cops?

Had she been murdered just for having Allen's card in her coin purse?

Cheryl's gaze shifted to the other body. This child—boy or girl? She didn't know. Whatever it was, it had been wearing yellow shorts and a red tank top on Friday in the laundromat. It had been dirty, and smelly, and whiny. But it certainly hadn't deserved to be found dead on Saturday afternoon, floating face down in Caddo Lake, still in the yellow shorts and red tank top.

She walked back up the bank. Royce Sims had just stopped his patrol car, and she greeted him with some relief. "Don't let anybody walk down the bank," she told him, "and don't let any of these people here leave. Hand me your mike."

On the radio, she asked for Tach 2. "Sergeant?" she said, after she was patched through to the detective bureau. "It's Lucille Brantley. And a hundred percent sure it's mixed up with the case Allen's been on. You might better tell McCain about it and see if he wants to come out here."

McCain wanted to come out there. So, very shortly, did two exceedingly weary lab technicians who'd driven from Memphis, Tennessee, to East Texas without any rest and who weren't used to working homicides. (Well, at least they were told they wanted to. Cheryl didn't hear anybody ask their opinion.) Detective Bert McAllister was told to remove to the detective bureau, for statements, both of the fishermen, Charlotte, and Waymon. Waymon protested loudly about freedom of the press. "Tough shit," McAllister told him. "Just think about what a story you'll have to tell now."

At the last minute, McCain detailed another postal inspector who'd driven to the lake with him, a tall gangly man who seemed to be called Red, to go help talk to the four witnesses. Then he looked at his watch and back up the bank. "I wonder what's keeping the lab," he muttered.

"They're probably lost," Cheryl said. "If you're not used to these lake roads it's easy to get lost."

McAllister had another short delay while the grey-haired fisherman got rid of his chewing tobacco, and while Charlotte, who had inadvertently glanced down at the lake again, was sick once more. But at last the witnesses left, all crammed together into one police car with the promise that yes, certainly they would all be brought back to their cars.

"Thank God," McCain said as they departed.

"Amen on that," Cheryl answered fervently.

"How many of them do you know?" McCain asked. "I can't get used to a place like this, where everybody seems to know everybody."

"I'd like to get used to a place where everybody doesn't know everybody," Cheryl answered. "I know three of the four."

"Oh?"

"Charlotte's my sister, and Waymon is her boyfriend. He's a sort of part-time reporter who thinks he's going to grow up to be Hemingway. The older fisherman I don't know; the younger is Terry Rhoads."

"Who's Terry Rhoads?"

"I'm sorry to say, the father of my daughter," Cheryl said tightly.

"I didn't know you'd been married," McCain said.

"I wasn't," Cheryl said, feeling herself blushing with fury as well as embarrassment. Why should he know? They'd just met that day.

" 'Scuse me," McCain said. "Didn't mean to pry. But sorry, I still need to ask. Who is he?"

"That's all you meant anyway," Cheryl realized. "All right. He's just a guy. His family's lived here as long as mine has—call it over a hundred years. He went to college with me in Commerce, got out and went into the service, came home and hasn't done much since. He's a charter pilot. I think he flies some dope, but I can't prove it. And he goes over to Shreveport to the horse races, and he fishes—here, Arkansas, wherever. He's flown some fishing trips to Alaska, oil men and that sort of thing." She shrugged. "That's really all there is to say. He's not your man, if that's what you're asking. He's usually a nice guy when he's sober. He's a devil when he's drunk. Hey, look, we've got a homicide to work. At least I do." Vaguely, she wondered where Terry had left Holly. In the nursery, probably.

"Yeah. Okay. And this is Lucille Brantley?" McCain asked.

"Yeah."

"You're sure?"

"Of course I'm sure."

McCain looked down at the corpse. "Damn! I did want to talk to her! If I could have found her, I was going to put her into protective custody, at least until this Darling Corey showed up."

"There's no way you could have reached Lucille alive," Cheryl told him.

"What do you mean?"

"Rigor's absolutely complete," Cheryl said. "The water, especially that shallow, isn't all that cool. I'd say she was dead before Allen was shot. And, I thought last night it was just bad luck that we drove in on them. I don't now. I think now they were waiting for him."

Not seeing any connection at all between the two crimes, McCain asked, "How do you know rigor's complete?" He could not visualize Cheryl Burroughs going into Caddo Lake to handle a corpse.

But Cheryl misunderstood the question. "How do you—" she began to repeat, and then stopped. "Oh, of course, you're not used to working homicides. You just check, that's all. It starts in the chest, spreads first to the jaw area, and reaches the extremities last. If the wrists and ankles are completely stiff, especially in someone as big as Lucille was, it's not going to be much under twelve hours and could be as much as eighteen. The extent of post-mortem lividity—that staining that looks like bruises on the underside of the body—suggests the same. Of course there are a lot of variables, but most of them apply when the victim is in poor physical condition, or the environment is cold, or death is virtually instantaneous. And none of these are true here." She glanced at the body again. "Especially not that last."

"If it was eighteen—" McCain stopped and figured. "That would put it around nine o'clock last night."

"Right," Cheryl said. "And I really do think it was close to eighteen hours. So whoever it was—Oh, damn, they've got to have been watching Allen to kill her and then try to kill the man she might have talked to. And if they knew where to wait for him, and even what time to wait for him, they had to have been watching him for several days."

"How long had he been going out there at night?"

"I don't know. Didn't he tell you?"

"He told me, yes. What I want to know is how much he told you, and how long ago he told you, and maybe who else might have known." The tone of McCain's voice was icy.

Cheryl swallowed. Allen had told her to do her best to cooperate with this man, but it wasn't going to be easy, not if he was going to come out with questions that assumed she was a scatterbrained child. She said clearly, "Last night before we went to the movie, Allen mentioned that he was going to that post office afterwards. That didn't leave me time to tell anyone, even if I had wanted to. Good grief, Mr. McCain, I've been in police work for six years! Even if I'd had a chance, which I didn't, and even if I didn't have any regard for security, which I do, I wouldn't have risked Allen getting hurt!"

"I didn't mean to imply you were at fault," McCain said stiffly. "It was Conyers I had in mind. I don't know who else he might have told. Whether you know it or not, he's been under some severe emotional strain. I don't think his reaction to it would take the form of confiding about his work to strangers, but—"

"But you're not sure. No, Mr. McCain, it only takes the form of being very interested in and concerned about other people's children."

"Then you do know."

"Yes, I do. And I'm the only person in Caddo County who does. Kindly have the decency to leave it that way. I'm sure that if Allen wants other people to know his personal problems he'll be glad to tell them himself." She looked at the lake. "I'd hate him to see this," she added. "Yesterday, at the laundromat, he bought that child a candy bar."

"Did Lucille tell you anything yesterday?"

And Allen would have already answered that, too, Cheryl thought. But McCain wants confirmation. I wonder why? I wonder if he thinks Allen really can't remember?

But she answered, "No, Lucille was scared. Allen said he'd talked to her a couple of times, and she seemed terrified out of her mind of the Man, as she called the suspect. I'm not sure she ever understood who Allen was. At first she was afraid he was from the Man, testing her out to see if she'd talk."

"She thought Allen was from the Man or was the Man?"

"Was from the Man. But I'm telling you hearsay now. She didn't tell me that; Allen did."

"I'll get it from Allen, then. And I wish you would quit calling me 'Mr. McCain' in that tone of voice. My name is Jim."

"And I wish you would quit assuming I am totally brainless," Cheryl replied. "I am not a rookie."

"That's clear. I don't always mean all I seem to imply; I'm not long on tact." He looked back at the body and gestured at the head. "The card. I thought Allen told me she threw it on the floor and refused to keep it."

"She did. But you know we're only assuming that it's the same card."

"What are you talking about? I can see from here that that's Allen Conyers's card."

"I know," Cheryl said, "but he's been handing them out fairly wholesale. There are a lot of Allen's cards floating around Caddo County. In other words, I'm saying that we've been assuming she picked the card back up off the floor and her killer found it on her. But that doesn't have to be the same card. Allen could have given a card to someone else and the killer could have got hold of it. Or Allen could even have given the killer a card. Because remember, we don't know who the killer is."

A perfectly preposterous hypothesis was beginning to grow in Jim McCain's mind. He wanted to tell it to somebody so that he could be told how preposterous it was. Only he didn't want to tell it to anybody because it couldn't be true, and he didn't want anybody else to think it. He didn't want to think it himself because it *was* perfectly preposterous.

But it had begun to grow in his mind that morning when he thought a couple of times that Allen was lying or maybe just skirting the truth for no apparent reason. It was still growing, and it wouldn't go away.

Whoever was working these jobs knew—damn it, he *knew!*—how post offices work. And whoever it was assembled a new crew everywhere he went, which said that he knew something about how to organize people and how to locate whores and make them do other work, and he knew how to pass checks, and he knew something about how to avoid leaving physical evidence—and how to—

And Allen Conyers had gone to Dallas two years back with a lot of leave saved up. He hadn't been taking much leave the last few years. And he was still nervous and upset about that messy divorce he refused to discuss, and he didn't like Dallas. The private letter that came with his transfer, the letter he didn't see, said to keep him busy, not to give him time to brood. But Allen hadn't, for a while, wanted to be busy. He'd liked East Texas, and Louisiana, and Arkansas—the whole area called the ArkLaTex—from the first time he was sent over there to work a check case. He kept asking for leave and rushing over to East Texas, or Northwest Louisiana, or Southwest Arkansas, to go fishing.

Well, he had the leave coming. They couldn't very well deny it to him. That was partly why, when the post in Lakeport opened up, they'd let him have it . . . because the inspector in charge knew, by that time, that at least half the leave time Allen had asked for on the grounds of fishing trips hadn't been spent fishing. It had been spent just hanging around the area, meeting people, getting to know the towns. And he hated Dallas, and he didn't like Fort Worth much better, and he was, he said, thoroughly sick of cities. But he explained that he sure did like the little towns around Caddo Lake.

He was on leave, alledgedly fishing in Arkansas, when the southwestern part of Arkansas was hit by three steady weeks of stolen and forged checks, followed by two mail truck heists and two post office robberies. And he was on leave, allegedly fishing in Louisiana, when—

No, that couldn't be true. He'd been shot with the same gun, for almost certain sure (although all that was really sure, McCain conscientiously reminded himself, was that it was the same make and caliber) as had the man in Bossier City, and he certainly didn't shoot himself. But on the other hand, there had been two people holding up that post office, and if one partner later thought the other might turn on him, he might—

It couldn't be true. Allen Conyers had been a postal inspector since—since before Jim McCain got out of high school. It couldn't be true anyway because if Cheryl was right about the timing—and she probably was—this woman had been tortured and stabbed to death while Cheryl and Allen were together. Unless Cheryl was lying, too. And if Cheryl was wrong, if it was closer to twelve hours than eighteen, then this woman had been killed when Allen Conyers was indisputably on the ground with a bullet in his gut.

Wait a minute, though. Cheryl was saying "at least" about the time. Suppose it wasn't "at least"? Suppose it was "at most"? How long could she stay stiff before decomposition began to set in? Could she have been dead—well, she'd been seen alive Friday at one o'clock. Had Allen and Cheryl really been together all afternoon? No, Cheryl had said something about taking a nap.

How long had this taken?

And how big an organization did this killer have? Big enough for him to get some work done while he was elsewhere, clearly, but this sort of work?

And if it wasn't Allen, how in the holy hell was the killer or his crew getting in and out of post offices without leaving a trail?

But if it was Allen, what reason would he have had? Well, he'd brooded a lot about that divorce. McCain didn't know the whole story, but he did know Conyers had been bitterly angry at the woman he'd divorced. Say, he went to really brooding on it—decided to blame all women and the post office (because probably his being away so much had been a contributing factor in his divorce)—but if that was true, why wasn't he mad at Cheryl?

And why, anyway, would he have killed a child? McCain didn't remember a child involved in the divorce; he remembered Conyers as childless. And what had Cheryl meant anyway about his interest in other people's children?

Well, that didn't matter. The point was, this murder could be explained.

But the other question was why would he have started it all to begin with, a man with that many years in law enforcement, a man with as good a work record as Conyers had. That was unanswerable. But that question was always asked when any trusted person anywhere went bad, and it was always unanswerable.

McCain didn't want to believe any of it. Most of all, he didn't want to believe anybody he knew had killed Matt Elton or even consented to his death. Especially not another postal inspector. There might be something in the world that could hurt Jim McCain worse than that, but just now he couldn't think what.

It couldn't be true. It was, of course, completely preposterous . . . but just to be on the safe side, for a while McCain was going to proceed as if it were true. Which would mean very largely playing a lone hand, because if he cooperated with the local police department (as he was supposed to do) every move he made would be known to Cheryl Burroughs, and every fact she knew would be known to Allen Conyers.

The lab technicians came walking down the bank. McCain hadn't heard the lab truck arrive. He had no idea how long he had been staring, unseeing, at the mutilated body of the dead woman.

One of the lab men looked as if he were considering being sick. "I didn't," he said, "think I'd contracted for corpses when I went to work for the post office." That couldn't be exactly true; one thing the lab worked was post office bombings and another was plane crashes if the plane was carrying mail.

The other, who'd been with the Los Angeles County Sheriff's Department Laboratory before going to the post office, didn't look in the least interested in being sick. He didn't even look particularly interested in the corpse. He just hooked the strobe to the side of the camera and began taking pictures.

After a while, the detective car returned with the two fishermen, Charlotte, and Waymon, all of whom were requested to please clear the area immediately. Terry, clearly not eager to see Cheryl, hastened to comply; the grey-haired fisherman did not walk back down the bank.

"But I'm a reporter," Waymon protested.

McCain started up the bank toward him. It was useful, Cheryl thought, to have his acid tongue to turn loose on Waymon. Waymon was getting to be a pest.

But she had counted without the pest's persistence. Thirty minutes later, just after the coroner arrived with the apologetic explanation that he was sorry to be so late but his beeper went out, Waymon appeared immediately offshore, without Charlotte but in his boat, taking pictures through a telephoto lens. And there wasn't a thing in the world anybody could do about that except fume, fret, and go on working.

When they finally turned the bodies over they found that yes, Lucille's hands had been tied behind her, and no, her child hadn't been drowned. He'd been stabbed, too.

"You stupid," Darling Corey said much later that night. "I tole you, anybody watches TV knows you shoots a fed, you gots more trouble than a dog gots fleas. You din' tell me it was no fed you wanted to shoot. Now you crying to me about how the place is lousy with feds. You stupid." She spread out her hands to give the nail polish time to dry. "You stupid, killing a baby," she added. "You don' needs to go killing no baby. Baby cain' tell who you is."

"It got in my way," her companion said sullenly. "And don't you go calling me stupid. Nobody calls me stupid. I shot a fed before and didn't get in no trouble."

"You don' want me to call you stupid, then don' be stupid. Don' shoot no more feds. Just 'cause they don' catch you one time, that don' mean they don' catch you. You wants to ride in my car again tonight?"

"No, I don't want to ride in your car. I wish I hadn't bought the damn thing. I'm half tempted to turn it back in for cash."

"Oh, baby!" Darling Corey protested. "You don' wants to do that." Nervously she twisted the silver bracelet around her wrist.

"Then don't call me stupid." He got up and walked around the room restlessly. He had no doubt that the police and the feds were hunting Darling Corey; he'd gotten out of Lucille, before she died, a confession that she'd mentioned to Allen Conyers that Darling Corey might have cashed some checks. He'd demanded to know what other names she'd given; she'd screamed in terror that there weren't any others, that was the only name she even knew. And apparently it was. If she'd known any other names, the man thought coldly, she'd have told him about them. Before she died.

But that was the difference between Lucille and Darling Corey. Lucille had always been afraid. He'd tried to make her more afraid of him than of anybody else, but she was most afraid of whoever was with her. And at least for a while, she'd been more afraid of the soft-voiced, soft-eyed—soft, he thought contemptuously—man who'd come around from the post office asking questions.

But he'd made her afraid of him, and he'd keep other people afraid of him. Yes, even post office people, just like he'd had to be afraid when he was a boy. But now he was big—he was the Man—and he was the unknown. Even the feds were afraid. Even in the dark he'd seen that burst of fear in Conyers's face even if he hadn't screamed like the other fed did.

People feared him, now. Even Darling Corey feared him.

But Darling Corey was different from the other whores; Darling Corey wasn't afraid of anybody or anything except him. But she was an avaricious gold digger. He didn't want to kill her. But if those feds ever got to her—

No, they couldn't bully any information out of her, and they wouldn't even if they could. She was right about that, he thought. Feds don't hit people. But buy? How much would they pay to know who shot Allen Conyers? Could she buy her way out of Lakeport into a big city and turn into an uptown whore? Because she'd never be more than a whore, no matter how much money she had—a beautiful, avaricious, murdering slut—that was all Darling Corey would ever be.

But he didn't have to kill her yet. He could keep her for a few more days, before she got too restless, before she got to demanding to go to the Amvet or the Silver Fox. For a day or two more she'd stay delighted by the stereo, and the big-screen television, and the carpet in the bathroom, and the waterbed, and all the other things he'd spent the money on so that it wouldn't show except to people he let in this secret house that was not where most people thought he lived at all.

Yes, he'd have to kill her. But he'd keep her to enjoy for a few more days. "Say, Darling Corey," he said, "make us a drink, would you?"

·*Five*·

He was still brooding on Sunday morning. The loss of Jimmy
Pitts hadn't, he'd now decided, been as disastrous as he'd first
thought. Of course Jimmie had been useful when he was making his initial arrangements in Arkansas. Jimmie taught him how to avoid doing
the kind of things people watch for—the really dumb things, like too
many or too few digits in a driver's license number, as well as the less
obvious things like being too jittery while waiting to cash a check. And
Jimmie had told him how you can sometimes (but not always) avoid
leaving fingerprints.

He'd been able to add to that what he'd learned from the locksmith
course he'd taken while he was in high school, and from his aunt who
worked at the post office, and from that holiday job he'd once had as
substitute mail sorter. All that had helped; and Jimmie knew the
whores and how to make them work. They'd made a good team at the
beginning.

But on the other side of the ledger, Jimmie had started wanting
more than his fair share of the profits. Even worse, he'd begun to
show an alarming tendency to go off on his own. That bank robbery,
now. Jimmie wasn't a hold-up man by profession; he was a con man,
and although he'd turned killer, it was mainly out of fear of being
caught.

It had been hard to talk him into the first post office robberies, the
ones in Arkansas. It had been easier to talk him into the one in
Louisiana.

But they'd agreed, just post offices because post offices (except
really big ones) rarely have guards, rarely have cameras, rarely have
people trained to pay attention to faces. They'd been thoroughly
masked at the post offices anyway. That had been hard to teach Jim-

mie, too. People don't notice con men's faces; Jimmie didn't see why they'd be any more likely to notice robbers' faces.

As a result, when Jimmie got drunk and decided to go off on his own and rob a bank, he hadn't noticed the cameras because he wasn't used to thinking about cameras. And he hadn't worn a mask because he didn't figure anybody would *really* remember his face. And then, when his picture turned up on the six o'clock news caught on film in the act of robbing a bank, he came running and asking for cover.

Well, the Man had hidden him, figuring on sending him away after the noise died down. But why didn't he just hide? He didn't have to go shooting at cops, not in the daytime when they could see him and have time to shoot back.

Well, luckily Darling Corey had sense enough to come to him, but now that stupid broad thought she could just waltz back into the Silver Fox like nothing had happened!

She was right about one thing, though. Shooting Allen Conyers, as fun as it was, might have been a mistake. But he hadn't realized. It was just bad luck that that inspector walked in that time in Bossier City; he hadn't planned, until then, to kill anybody. He'd been planning to back off as soon as he was clear, and let things cool and then start up some- where else, just as he had when he'd left Arkansas. He hadn't let the killing stop him from following his plan completely; he hadn't set foot in Louisiana since. And although he'd taken numbered money orders and that sort of thing, they were just to give the feds something to look for. He didn't plan on using them, at least not any time soon, although he'd kept them in case of need instead of following his original impulse to burn them.

But the point was, he hadn't gone back to Louisiana. His organiza- tion there was disbanded, his people were doing other things, and he'd had no idea of the flurry of activity following the robbery and shooting. He didn't know that for two months the streets of Bossier City were alive with federal agents and that six postal inspectors and four FBI agents and two Secret Service agents had all been out hunting the killer.

The killer didn't know because he hadn't been there.

And Jimmie had told him not too long after they first met that postal inspectors are smart, but that in most places (except big cities) there's just one, or at the worst, two of them. So, when he began to get worried that the trail to him in Lakeport might not be as well covered as he had planned, he figured it would be easy. Just kill the fed. Get rid of him and then finish up here and get gone before another one came along.

But then Conyers hadn't died, despite that fear in his eyes when the gun went off, despite the sirens the Man had heard later that night. That was the first surprise. A man as slow-moving, as soft-voiced, as easy-going as that man was ought not to be able to survive a well-placed bullet. But he had survived, and that meant even the little suspicions in his mind, the ones that hadn't even solidified enough for him to write them down, would still be followed up.

And the second surprise, the one he'd have expected if he'd stayed in Louisiana when he left, was even worse. That surprise was all the damn *feds*. It seemed like he couldn't go outside without seeing them. They were everywhere, in all the stores asking questions like, "Can you remember who cashed this check?" and in all the bars saying, "Hey, honey, come talk to me a minute; you need a five I'll get you one. Just tell me has anyone approached you about—"

And it wouldn't have mattered, in Louisiana, because none of them knew who he was. But here some of them did. Well, he'd made sure all the little whores knew what had happened to Lucille. The bitch! She'd tried to tell him she didn't talk to no postal inspector; he wouldn't even have known it was a lie except that dirty little brat was playing with the card. Then she tried to say the kid had picked it up off the floor, but when he asked how it got on the floor for the kid to pick up, she didn't have an answer. Not an answer he could accept, anyway. Not a good answer.

Now he sat brooding, wondering how much longer he could keep Darling Corey, and who he could replace her with when he got rid of her, and how he would get rid of her when the time came.

But how, and when, would be determined partly by how hard the police were hunting her, how much they wanted to find her. About that, he had no idea—he'd have to check into that.

Even if they weren't hunting her he'd eventually have to kill her. Because he couldn't take her along the way he'd told her he could. He'd take along the other girl, the clean one, the one he'd watched and made sure stayed clean just for him.

Darling Corey wasn't clean. She was a whore. She looked like a whore. He looked at her approvingly. That was how he wanted her to look.

"A girl like this ought to be able to take care of herself, anyway," Jim McCain commented. Lone hand or no, there was no way he could get hold of Darling Corey's file without the local police knowing he had it. So there was no way to handle the matter except to go and ask for the file, and discuss the file, and do his best to act like there was nothing on his mind he couldn't share. Looking, now, at the file, he asked, "How the hell did she get an acquittal on two separate shootings?"

"You tell me," Hall answered, "because I damn sure can't tell you."

"And these are all her mug shots?" McCain asked, surveying them glumly. He picked out three from the selection. In most of those available, Darling Corey was smiling at the camera. And she was, undeniably, a pretty woman, milk chocolate skin, very large deep brown eyes. The shoulder-length hair in one picture was in a pageboy that made her look almost like an ordinary business woman. In the second, she was more dramatic and less conventional; her hair was a huge feathery Afro, and she was wearing enormous carved ivory earrings. A third McCain picked out as possibly more representative had caught her in a worse moment. She'd clearly been in a fight. Her lips, firmly closed, were swollen, and there was blood on her face. "Hey, what happened here?" he asked, not expecting anyone to know.

But Lloyd readily answered. "Oh, that was the night she and Cheryl got in it. Cheryl was trying to arrest her, and she didn't want to be arrested. So she broke Cheryl's wrist, and Cheryl broke her front teeth."

"Oh," McCain said, for want of anything better to say. "But I sure do wish you had a few full-length, or even some showing a height scale."

"You just got to ask," Hall said reproachfully. "We don't keep those with the regular mug shots. Just a sec." He went into his inner office and came back with four photos. Two were done in available light and were a little grainy; they showed Darling Corey, Lucille Brantley, and a couple of other women in, apparently, a nightclub. The other two were posed photos, front and profile, by a height scale. "These," McCain said, pointing to the other women in the nightclub. "Who?"

"That one's Clareise Hopkins. I'll have to spell it for you; you'd never figure it out from the sound. The other's Mary Jane Rowe. And if you're thinking about questioning them, let's see." Hall frowned at the photo. "No, Clareise moved out of town about, oh, maybe a year ago. Mary Jane used to hang out at the Silver Fox. I'm not sure I've got a current address for her, but we ought to be able to locate her fairly easily."

"Can you loan me somebody?" McCain asked. "I need to get a person who's good at putting nicknames and names together and can help me locate these women."

"It would be best for you to use Cheryl," Hall answered, "since she's already been on this so much with Allen. I'll just pull her off regular calls unless something comes up and there's flat nobody else available. She's scheduled off today, but she's already called once and asked if she could come on in and work."

It was on the tip of McCain's tongue to say he didn't want Cheryl. But then he realized he couldn't. He'd been rude about Cheryl Saturday, and Hall had been thoroughly annoyed about it. Because of that he couldn't say he didn't want Cheryl without sounding prejudiced against policewomen. Which maybe he was, but rules being what they were, he knew he had to keep any prejudices he might have to himself.

The only other solution would be to give the real reason for not wanting Cheryl. And that he couldn't do. There was too big a chance he was wrong.

And God, how he wanted to be wrong this time.

"Yeah, call her in if you're really sure she won't mind working with me," he said. He could just ask her not to tell Allen on the grounds that he shouldn't be thinking about work. But she'd probably tell him anyway.

McCain became aware of a raging headache.

"I wonder," he said slowly, after Hall got back from the telephone, "if this killing of Lucille fits into the pattern anywhere?"

"You can always check it out," Hall answered.

Hopewell Springs, the town in Arkansas, was small. Bossier City, a suburb of Shreveport, was not so small and could easily have a spillover from Shreveport's metropolitan type of trouble. A dead whore there might not mean much. He decided to call Hopewell Springs first.

The chief of police there, a man named Ed Lewis, was cooperative, although a little puzzled as to why a postal inspector out of Fort Worth, currently located in Lakeport, needed to know whether a whore had been killed in Hopewell Springs nineteen months earlier. "Well, let's see," he said, "it seems to me—but you want to know exactly if it happened the same week the post office was stuck up?"

"Or about—oh, say three weeks either side of that."

"Just let me check. Hold on." Shortly, he was back on the phone, saying apologetically, "No, we had one about two years ago, but it was more than five months before the stickup."

"Can you do one more thing for me?" McCain asked.

"Yeah, whatever you need."

"How many hotels and motels do you have in town?"

Lewis laughed wryly. "Little Rock we're not. There's two. One's really a truck stop with cubes and showers where the truckers spend their stopovers, and then there's the Starlight Courts. It's got about six or eight cabins."

"Can you get me a list of everybody who stayed at either one of them for over three days the month of the robbery?"

"I can tell you right off nobody stays over one day at the truck stop. They don't have rooms there; they have cubes, and they rent them by the hour. And before you ask, no, I can't tell you working girls don't hang out there. I don't worry about them as long as nobody gets rolled. The Starlight—let's see, I got that at the time; it should be still around. Hold on."

He was back in three minutes with a rather short list of names. Jimmie Pittman was one; quite possibly that was really Jimmie Pitts, and if so, it would seem to confirm their suspicion that Pitts was involved with—well, with whoever the perpetrator was. McCain didn't recognize any of the other names, although he wrote them all down, until the last one.

Allen Conyers.

Allen Conyers stayed at the Starlight Courts for two weeks in December, eighteen months ago.

Why didn't we notice, McCain asked himself, when he kept taking leave. He wasn't fishing. You don't go fishing for two weeks in December in Hopewell Springs, Arkansas.

Who had they sent to Arkansas when all that mess erupted there—Whittier? Where was Whittier now? He'd been transferred, but where to? Have to find him, and ask if he knew—

Hall was going to be wondering what was wrong if he didn't say something soon. For that reason, not really much caring about the answer, he asked, "Did you get hold of Cheryl?"

"Uh-uh, not yet. That's what I was going to tell you, when you decided to get on the phone. There wasn't any answer at her apartment, and the hospital said she hadn't gotten there yet. I figure I'll call again in about ten minutes."

"Don't bother," McCain said, "I think I'll drive over there." Somebody else, he thought. There's got to be somebody else if it was Allen Conyers and Jimmie Pitts, because somebody ambushed Conyers after Pitts was dead. Somebody scared, maybe? Somebody who thought Conyers wanted out and had killed Pitts to get rid of one of the people who could identify him, somebody who was scared he'd be next?

Somebody, maybe, who was right?

It didn't seem so preposterous, not any more. I'm going to ask him about Arkansas, McCain decided. He'll have an explanation of why he was there, no matter what the reason is. If he's innocent, and maybe he is, it'll make sense. If he's not, well, it'll still make sense because he's not a stupid man, but he'll get a little shook up whether he shows it or not.

It is unnecessarily cruel to try to worry a badly injured man. But if he's innocent this won't worry him; if he's innocent he won't even notice that there's any reason why these questions should worry him. And if he's guilty, McCain thought, if he is guilty, well, then I don't care how wounded he is.

Cheryl was sitting by Allen's bed and from the grim look on Allen's face, Jim McCain surmised they'd been talking about Lucille Brantley.

"Cheryl just told me about Lucille Brantley," Allen said to McCain. He sounded exhausted and extremely angry. "I feel—damn! I feel like it's my fault, but there was no reason why giving my card to her should have gotten her killed."

"It's not your fault, Allen," Cheryl said. "And as much as I hate to say it, any girl in her line of work has a lot greater chance of winding up murdered than other people do. If it hadn't been for that card, I might even be inclined to call it coincidence."

"Well, it wasn't," Allen said and looked at McCain. "What did you come over about? Has something else come up?"

McCain had been wondering, all the way over, how he was going to ask for an alibi for Lucille's killing without letting Allen realize that was what he was asking for. Now inspiration struck. "Two things, actually," he said. "Well, make it three. I need to borrow Cheryl today."

Allen nodded. "That's one. But it's not up to me."

"Cheryl, your boss okayed it if you feel up to it."

"Okay," Cheryl said, not too enthusiastically. Not, McCain thought, liking him much at all.

"Next thing," McCain said, "is because I got to thinking about something Cheryl said yesterday. She thinks you may have been followed."

"Friday? I don't think so," Allen said.

"That's not quite what I said anyway," Cheryl interrupted. "I said they might have been watching him at different times, but I didn't necessarily mean Friday."

"Well, let's think about it anyway. Let's go back to when Jimmie Pitts was shot and pick it up there. Let me try to get an exact timetable in my mind. After the shooting, you both got hauled off to the hospital in an ambulance. Then?"

"Then we sat up there for about two hours and finally got bandaged. Ken Hall drove Cheryl and me back to the police station to give statements about what happened. Then I got Hall to drive me over to the car rental place in Longview. He offered to loan me a detective's car, but I didn't want to borrow it. He doesn't have enough anyway."

"Go on," McCain said.

"Then I went home. I was pretty dirty and had a lot of blood on my shirt. I felt like an idiot going to the rental agency that way, but obviously I had to have wheels. When I got home, I tried to figure out how to take a shower without getting the bandage wet. Finally I held a trash bag over the bandage long enough to get cleaned up."

"Ingenious," Cheryl said. "I didn't think of that."

"Not very ingenious," Allen answered. "I got the bandage wet anyway. So then—I wasn't hungry, but I thought I'd better eat something. So I made a sandwich and drank a glass of milk with it—you don't want all this, do you?"

" 'Fraid I do."

"I don't see why."

"Tell you later. I do have a reason."

Allen tried, not very successfully, to shrug. "Well, okay. So then, I tried to read for a while but I was still too jumpy to read. Then I called Cheryl to see if I could go over to her house for a while. She said I could, and on the way I stopped by a liquor store and bought a half pint of Seagram's. I had one drink and stayed—how long, Cheryl, about forty-five minutes? I guess it was about nine when I left there.''

"And then?''

"And then I went to Caddo Springs and sat inside the post office.''

"How did you approach it? I mean when you got there, not the road you took.''

"I drove all the way around the building and then parked on the right, near the back, up against the side of the building.''

"Just about where the sedan was parked Friday night?''

"Just about, yes.''

"And somebody could have seen you parked there if they'd driven around too? Would you have seen a car do that?''

"If it had its lights on I'd have seen it from where I was. If the headlights were off, no, probably not.''

"Is that where you usually parked when you went out there?'' I may really be on to something, McCain thought. Maybe he really was followed. Even if he's in it himself, he didn't plan to be ambushed.

"Yes,'' Allen said.

"Then why didn't you drive all the way around the building Friday night?''

"I don't know,'' he said. "Maybe it was because I felt invulnerable. I had Cheryl with me.''

"Oh, Allen,'' Cheryl said, sounding shocked, distressed, and flattered all at once.

"It wasn't your fault,'' he answered. "I just didn't think. I'll admit it was quite a price to pay for not thinking, but it could have been worse.''

"Yeah,'' McCain said. "But back to your timetable. What time did you finally leave Caddo Springs?''

"About five-thirty.''

"After telling me at nine you were going to go home and go to bed!'' Cheryl exclaimed.

"I finally did. I got to bed about six A.M., slept till, oh, around ten. Then I went to the police station after I shaved and finished waking up.''

"And then?''

"Then I waited for Cheryl to come in. She got there, oh, call it eleven-fifteen.'' He went on through the day, detailing time spent.

Finally McCain asked, "All right, then you took Cheryl back to the police station. What time was that?"

"Around five."

And this was the time McCain had really been aiming at. Not that he would tell the truth, if it had been him, but maybe he'd act a little jumpy. "Then what?" he asked casually.

"Then I went home. I watched the six o'clock news on TV, read the paper a little, slept about an hour, and went back out and got Cheryl around eight. We went to Watson's for dinner and then we went to the drive-in. Do you need any more from there on?"

"No, we've been over the rest of it adequately." Nothing that could be proved, of course. Three hours not accounted for by anybody but himself. Was that enough time to mutilate and kill a woman, kill a child, and dump the bodies in the lake?

Where would it have happened? And how did anyone, no matter who it was, transport them without getting blood all over his car? But memory answered both those questions. Lucille had been killed in her own house. And the thick black garbage bags the bodies had been moved in were wrapped around the cypress trees below the bodies.

He hadn't acted nervous, hadn't seemed to feel that any one time was any more important than any other. Damn it, I'm paranoid, McCain thought. He couldn't have done it. Not this man. I know this man.

If he just hadn't been in Hopewell Springs those two weeks.

"Why were you in Hopewell Springs December a year ago?" he asked bluntly.

"Helping Whittier," Allen replied easily. "He'd asked for help and the head shed said it wasn't necessary. But this was his first big case by himself and he was feeling pretty desperate. So I took leave—said I was going fishing, I think—and went on over to help out some. Why?"

"I just wondered. I was checking today on who was there, and was a little surprised to find your name came up."

"Yeah," Allen said. And then he asked, slowly, "What kind of a bee have you got in your bonnet?" Now he'd guessed; his lips were tightening into a firm line.

"Nothing," McCain said. "Nothing, Allen, I just had to ask."

Now Cheryl, too, had realized the drift of the questions. Her eyes were furious, but she didn't say anything. It was Allen who said quietly, "Cheryl, please take a walk. I may be about to lose my temper, and if I do, what I'm likely to say I'm not sure I want to say in front of you."

She got up and walked out the door. She didn't quite slam it.

"Jim, what are you suspecting me of doing?" Allen asked, still very quietly.

"I never really tried to put it into words," McCain said. "And I'm trying not to suspect you. But I'm just curious. I just wondered, that's all."

"Then tell me what it is you wondered. I think I have the right to know."

"I suppose you do," McCain said. "All right. Point. Whoever is doing this can get in and out of post offices easily, has at least a certain amount of knowledge of physical evidence, and has considerable organizational ability."

"I'm not sure I have any organizational ability, but I'll agree that the other two points fit. Go on."

"He is emotionally disturbed. I'm not saying you are, but I think we all know you've been under considerable emotional stress the last few years."

"From which I am now substantially recovered, but I'll concede that for a while, four to five years ago, I might have qualified as at least slightly emotionally disturbed."

"I don't know the reason for your divorce, but whatever it was, it left you extremely bitter toward your ex-wife. This bitterness could have carried over to women in general."

"It didn't, but I can see that from your point of view, not knowing the situation, it could appear that way."

"You were in Hopewell Springs during the crime wave there. You were registered in the same hotel as Jimmie Pittman for about two weeks."

"And you think Jimmie Pittman was Jimmie Pitts?"

"It's possible."

"It is possible. But if he was, I either never saw him or never noticed him."

"You were in Bossier City just before their trouble started, and you were allegedly fishing at Caddo Lake when Matt Elton was shot." And that was just a guess. All he really knew was that Allen had been on leave nearby. But Allen merely nodded as McCain went on. "I've counted up. You spent a total of four months in the ArkLaTex area, using saved-up leave time, in the last two years. Most of that time you said you were fishing. And you weren't.''

"You're right. I wasn't.''

"Then what in the holy hell were you doing, Allen? For four months?''

"Developing sources. Developing snitches. That's all, mostly. I was trying to get so damn buried in my work I wouldn't see the world go by, and all anybody was giving me was penny-ante cases, and everybody kept watching me like they were afraid I was going to break. Well, I wasn't. I was angry and hurt when I left New York, but that doesn't mean I was either suicidal or murderous. I was, and am, neither.'' He tried to sit up in bed, grunted with pain, and lay back down, pushing a pillow under his head and then doubling it to give him a little more height. Then he went on.

"We got all economy-minded a few years back,'' he said. "We shut all the little one- and two-man offices. We consolidated. We got efficient. Well, I don't think we got efficient any way except financially and maybe mechanically. We lost a lot of our rapport with the local law enforcement officers. We lost about all of our snitches. So—you want to know where I spent my leave? All that leave I had saved up?''

"That's why I'm asking,'' McCain said, not very patiently.

"I spent it in police stations and sheriff's offices,'' he said, "and I spent it in bars and honky-tonks. I spent it working. Of course I can't prove a word of that. I never expected to have to. But no, I didn't meet Jimmie Pitts and set up a scheme to get rich and then shoot him to keep him from talking. And no, I wasn't shot by some other ex-partner who was scared I'd get him, as I guess you were thinking too. And God knows I didn't shoot Matt Elton. Jim, you ought to remember that two hours after he was shot I was in the Shreveport post office asking what I could do to help.''

McCain did remember and had thought about it. But, he'd thought, if you were trying to hide your trail, what better way was there to do it than to offer to follow it yourself?

Allen shook his head. "I can't prove any of it. And I guess I would have had time, between letting Cheryl out at the police station at five and picking her up at eight, to kill Lucille Brantley and her child and dispose of the bodies if I worked really fast, but I didn't. I didn't do any of it, Jim. All I did was my job, the best way I know how to do it. I know you'll have to go on and check all of this out, but I hate to see you wasting your time on me when the person who butchered Lucille Brantley is still on the street. And the person who shot me, too, if that matters.''

"It matters," McCain said. "I'm sorry, Allen. I'm sorry as hell. But can you see why I was looking at you, just a little?"

"Actually, I can," Allen said. "But it would be interesting to see you trying to explain it to Cheryl."

"God," McCain said. "I was going to ask her for help."

"You already did ask. I heard you."

Cheryl opened the door. "May I come back in?" she asked, her voice noticeably chilly.

"Yes," Allen said, "we got it straightened out."

"I'm going," McCain said. "Cheryl, when you're ready, I'll be downstairs in the lobby."

"Uh-huh," Cheryl said.

After he left, Allen held out his hand to Cheryl. "It's okay," he said gently. "There was a reason why he was looking at me. I expect he'll go on looking until he's got it all cleared up, but it's nothing to worry about. It's not a frame or anything like that. He wants to get the right person as bad as you and I do."

"I don't have to like it," Cheryl said resentfully.

"I don't have to like it either. And I don't like it. But I know what's evidence, and so do you. During the last two years, I've taken off on leave several times and lied about what I was doing and by coincidence this killer and I have been in the same place at the same time on a couple of occasions. The only reason I was lying was because I wanted to work on something they didn't want me to work on, but all the same I was lying, and now the lies have caught up with me. I just now told him what I was really doing, but since I lied once, he can't be sure I'm not lying now. So don't be mad at him. He's doing his job. Go help with it."

"Okay," Cheryl said. "If you say so."

"And don't worry about me. Just go find that dude before he kills somebody else."

"Okay," Cheryl said.

"And be careful."

"Don't *you* worry about *me*."

In the car, McCain asked, "Do you know Mary Jane Rowe?"

· 89 ·

"Yeah," Cheryl said remotely, gazing out the right window of the car.

"Where'd she likely be at this time of day?"

"Ten-thirty? She'd likely be asleep. And don't ask me in whose bed because I'm no psychic."

"The last record on her shows her address as 209 Fallin Court, but Hall says he doesn't think that's current."

"It's not current," Cheryl said. "She moved over on Mulberry —1201, I think—but she's probably not there any more either. What do you want her about? Has she been idented as one of the check passers?"

"No, but if Darling Corey and Lucille both were and she hangs around with them, I figure it's an even chance she's one, too. You know this town; I don't. If you were looking for her, where would you start?"

"With John Arnold. She cashes her welfare checks there mostly."

"Who's John Arnold?"

Cheryl didn't feel like playing guessing games this time. She gave a succinct explanation of who John Arnold was.

"That's interesting," McCain said. He didn't say anything else; he just drove to John Arnold's store, belatedly wondering aloud when he was nearly there whether it would be open on Sunday morning.

The store was open, but John Arnold wasn't there. His daughter Eileen, twenty-two and pregnant, was. "Dad went out of town," she said.

"Where out of town?" McCain asked.

"I don't know. Just out of town. He does that sometimes." She paused long enough to ring up a sack of potato chips and two candy bars for a teenaged girl. Unusually for this neighborhood, the girl was white; she had stringy dishwater blonde hair and a round, very fair face. "You'll get cavities," Eileen told the girl. "And pimples. And fat." The girl giggled.

"That's her lunch," Eileen told Cheryl. "Her mama works her butt off cleaning schools to get that girl lunch money, and that's what she buys for lunch. I don't know why Daddy goes on trying in this neighborhood. No," she said a moment later, "I haven't seen Mary Jane Rowe in, oh, about six months. That doesn't mean she's not been here, though, because since I got married I don't get over here except when Dad is really hurting for help."

"How often does your dad go out of town like this?" McCain asked.

"Just now and then."

"And he doesn't leave a forwarding address?"

"He calls once a day."

"Oh? But no forwarding address?"

"I just said that," she answered impatiently, putting catsup and potato chips into a sack.

"Thanks, Eileen. Jim, let's get on." Outside, Cheryl asked furiously, "*Now* what bee have you got in that bonnet? First Allen, now John. Don't you trust anybody?"

"Right now, frankly, no," McCain answered coldly. "And that includes you. And Hall. And sometimes even myself. Because all of us are too likely to go and confide in people, and if they just happen to turn out to be the wrong people—"

"Just for your information," she interrupted, "I don't confide in people about police business. And neither does Kenneth Hall. And neither does Allen Conyers. And as for you, I wouldn't tell you how to get across the street if Allen didn't want me to cooperate with you even after you started this nonsense of suspecting him."

She got in, slammed the car door, and went on. "By the way, I can tell you where John Arnold almost certainly is. He's looked up to in this community, and he wants to continue to be. But every now and then he's had all the baloney he can stand, and when he feels that way, he goes over to Shreveport and goes on a bender. And then he stays in a motel until he sobers up, and then he comes home."

"And so, of course, every time he goes out of town and nobody knows where he is, he's definitely and surely gone to Shreveport to get drunk?"

"I don't go to Shreveport and look after him," Cheryl answered, "so I suppose that from your point of view I don't know that that's true. There, now you have the answer you want. Gee, now, let's see how you could work it out. I've got it! You could say that Allen and John and Jimmie Pitts had a three-way coalition, and Jimmie got greedy and so Allen shot him. Oh, no, that won't work, because it was me who shot Jimmie Pitts. Well, actually, Allen shot him too, but it was me that killed him."

She didn't even notice McCain's astonished expression; she charged on. "Oh, well, you could say Allen set it up for me to. He so carefully arranged that Jimmie would start shooting at us, to give him a good excuse, you see. And then John and Allen, both of whom love kids, murdered Lucille and her baby, and John put them in the lake while Allen came over to pick me up to take me to the movie, *in* the same clothes he'd worn all day. Isn't it smart that he didn't get blood on them? Because I got up at six this morning to go to the autopsy, and whether you know it or not, there wasn't a teacup full of blood left in that woman's body. But Allen's so clever! He can't take a shower without getting his bandage wet, but butchering a woman while he's wearing his grey suit is a snap."

She unpinned one of her braids to tighten it and went on, talking around bobbypins held between her teeth. "So then John got worried that Allen would doublecross him after all that, so he sneaked out to Caddo Springs and waited for Allen to show up. And then John, being one of the best shots in Texas, and habitually using a .45, decided to shoot Allen with a .32 and did not succeed in killing him. Congratulations! You've got it all solved! Now you can go back to Fort Worth. Good-bye." The tears in her eyes were of sheer rage.

McCain pulled over to the side of the road, braked violently, and shouted, "That's enough, damn it! You think I *like* suspecting someone I care about?"

"When did you start caring about Allen?" Cheryl asked. "You certainly didn't seem to care much this morning when you spent about forty-five minutes trying to cross-examine him, with him doing his best to cooperate with you and hurting so bad it was an effort for him to get out three consecutive words."

"What the hell are you talking about? He's got medication for pain."

"He's got it, but he's not taking it."

"Why?"

"Because, if you'll recall, somebody murdered one of his snitches. And he's trying to go back over everything he's done since he got to town to see if he can find anything he might have missed that would give him an indication of who it was. He doesn't figure he could think well enough doped up to do paperwork. You've got all his original notes, you and the people who came with you, but he's got Xeroxed copies of all of them."

"Where'd he get them?"

"I took them to him."

"Where did *you* get them?"

"I Xeroxed them in Dallas, while I was waiting for the firearms comparison, before I gave them to you." She didn't add that she'd made two sets of copies.

"Good lord," McCain said. "Okay. I know you're mad, but try to hear me through. I don't really suspect Allen. It's just that he'd done a couple of things that look sort of funny. Maybe I'm seeing them out of context. But until those things are cleared up, I've got to go on regarding him as at least a halfway possible suspect."

"Why have you got to?"

"There have been crooked cops before now," McCain said. "The circumstances with Allen would be distinctly suspicious if anybody in any other profession were in that situation. So if I fail to treat them as suspicious in his case, then I am showing undue favoritism toward him because he is both a person I know and a member of my own profession. See what I mean?"

"I guess so," she said reluctantly.

"Cheryl, have you ever had to work on a case where the main suspect was another cop?"

"Yes," she said after a moment of silence.

"How'd you feel?"

"It was horrible at first," she said, "because I knew how the evidence looked, and so did he; he couldn't *not* know. And he acted frantic, and I didn't know if he was frantic because he was guilty and had been caught, or because he was innocent and had been set up. And he kept trying not to be mad at me and that made it even worse because if he wasn't mad I couldn't be. But then when I finally decided he'd really done it, I just felt like he should have known better. But I still felt rotten about it."

"Then try to imagine how I feel right now," McCain said. "I don't really think Allen's involved in this. I damn sure don't want to believe he is. If he should turn out to be, I'll feel, as you put it, rotten. You, I've no doubt, will feel even worse. But if he is, then it'll be just what you said—he should have known better." He started the car again. "When he picked you up to go to the movie, he was wearing the same clothes he'd worn all day?"

"Yes."

"Nobody told me that."

"You didn't ask."

"That's true," he said, "I didn't ask. I didn't ask because I didn't want anybody to know any suspicion of Allen had even crossed my mind. What's been said today between you and me needs to stay between you and me. There's no need to worry Allen with it, and I don't want Hall to know. I haven't told any of my crew, either. And I'm not going to."

Her relief was quite visible. "I thought they all must know," she said. "Are you still suspicious of John?"

"Not suspicious per se, just curious. Mr. Big, whoever he is, could easily be a person like John."

"That's true," Cheryl said. "Only I know it isn't John." She looked, unseeing, out the window.

McCain didn't mind the silence. He was not feeling happy about that latest bit of information Cheryl had given him. True, it made sense. Allen wanted to go over his paperwork so he didn't take medication because he didn't want to be too doped up to read. But how much reading and thinking could he do if he was hurting? It would also make sense for a man to refuse medication if he had something he had to be absolutely certain he didn't say, something he had to hide, because of a fear that opiates might reduce his ability to control his tongue, might let him betray himself.

"I have an idea," Cheryl said suddenly. "Allen was lots closer to the car than I was. He could have seen a lot more than I could. Have you thought of hypnotizing him, having him look at it as a movie and take it a frame at a time? And then you'd know he's telling the truth, too."

"People will lie under hypnosis if they've made up their minds to it firmly enough," McCain answered. "And I don't know if he can be hypnotized right now, in as much pain as he's in, and if he's treated for the pain he won't be able to concentrate enough for hypnosis. But it's sure as hell worth a try. Wonder where we can find somebody to do it?"

"Neal Ryan," Cheryl said. "He's a Ranger. And he's had all kinds of training in hypnotizing witnesses. If you want to stop at a phone, I'll call him."

"You better call Allen first and be sure he's willing."

"He'll be willing," Cheryl said confidently.

"Call anyway."

Allen was willing, and Ryan said, "I've been trying to find an excuse to get in on this shindig. Clear it with his doctor, and I'll meet you at the hospital at one o'clock."

·Six·

The hospital in Lakeport, built in 1942, looked older than it was. The stucco interior walls had been painted over repeatedly; at the moment they were a somewhat depressing pinkish beige. Nobody had thought to send Allen any flowers; he had a newspaper, one old paperback book, and a television he didn't seem at all interested in watching. He had the sheet and a light blanket pulled up to his waist. His chest was bare, and some of the adhesive tape from the bandages on his abdomen was visible. Cheryl wondered, briefly, whether he was wearing anything at all except the bandages, but remembering the discomfort of the clothes people are expected to wear in hospitals, she thought it would be quite reasonable if he wasn't.

The room was cool, but Allen's face was filmed with perspiration. Cheryl wondered whether he had a fever or whether the perspiration was the result of pain. But she didn't ask; she sat silently as Neal explained how hypnosis works, how it is often used to help witnesses and victims remember things they have pushed out of their conscious minds.

"Are you sure this will work?" Allen asked dubiously.

Neal, a rather bookish looking man whose only concession to the original meaning of "Ranger" was his hand-tooled leather boots, answered, "No, I'm not sure. It's really up to you. If you're willing and able to concentrate and relax, and if you really want it to work, then it will."

"I'm willing enough," Allen said, "but I'm not too confident of being able to relax. I'll try."

"I need the room cleared now," Neal said. "Allen, you decide who can come back in once I'm ready to ask questions."

"Everybody," Allen said. "I've got nothing to hide."

The room slightly darkened, the nurses' station warned of the hypnosis session in progress, Neal began talking quietly. Allen had been expecting to be told to stare at something, but all he was asked to do was listen.

He was vaguely aware that his breathing was deeper, more even. The room felt cooler, and he was oddly drowsy; his shoulders and legs seemed to feel heavy. He'd been so tense and so on guard for so long that he half expected the pain to overwhelm him when he began to relax, but it didn't. For a minute or two he was moaning softly with every breath, but then he was outside the pain. The pain was still present, he was still aware of it, but it no longer seemed a part of him.

And then he was no longer aware of it or of anything else.

To Cheryl, entering the room, he looked greatly rested. The deep lines the last few days had put in his face were scarcely visible.

Neal, sitting beside the bed, said, "Allen, can you hear me?"

"Yes." The word was very slightly slurred.

"Do you know where you are now?"

"Hospital."

"Why?"

"Someone shot me."

"Who?"

"I don't know."

"Where were you yesterday at this time?"

"Hospital."

The hypnotist went on, quietly moving him backward hour by hour, until they reached six o'clock on the day of the shooting. Neal asked, "Where are you now?"

"At home. The television is on. I'm watching the news."

"What channel?"

"It's on the cable. I don't know; it's a Dallas station. The newscaster has gotten her hair cut. She looks cooler now. Her hair was too thick for summer."

Cheryl looked around triumphantly at McCain; clearly Allen couldn't have been simultaneously watching the news and murdering Lucille Brantley.

"Now it's seven o'clock, same day. What are you doing?"

"Asleep on the couch."

"Move on forward; move forward to ten o'clock. What are you doing now?"

"Movie. With Cheryl."

"Let's go on to one A.M. Where are you?"

"In the car. I'm at Caddo Springs. I'm just stopping the car."

"All right," Neal said, "now you're watching a movie of what happened. You can see yourself, you can see everything you saw that night, but you won't feel anything. Understand?"

"Uh-huh. I'm watching a movie."

"You're watching a movie of yourself getting out of the car. Can you see it?"

"Uh-huh."

"Tell me what happens."

"I get out of the car. I take my keys out of my pocket. I'm walking toward the back of the post office. It's too dark; I ought to have a flashlight—what's that car doing there?" Restlessness was evident, and his face was heavily beaded with sweat. The surface of his subconscious might be willing to agree that he was watching a movie, but a deeper part of his mind knew quite well what the meaning of the movie was.

"It's all right, Allen. You won't feel anything," Neal said quickly. "Watch it as a series of slides, now, not as a movie. Let's take one slide at a time. What do you see first?"

"Car."

"Keep looking at the car. What color is it?"

"It's a white car."

"Can you see its license plate?"

"No. I see its side. I see its right front fender. There's a big dent in it. It drives like it's out of line. I think he hit something."

"Did you see him hit something?"

"No. But the car drives like it hit something. It's badly out of line."

"Do you know what make of car it is?"

"Plymouth or Dodge. Valiant maybe."

"How old a car is it?"

"Nine or ten years. It's not new."

"Now the car is nearer to you. What do you see?"

"He's got a gun."

"Can you see who it is that has the gun? Remember, it's just a slide. Who has the gun?"

"I can't tell. There's fire. I can't see past the fire." The anguish in his voice was nakedly real.

"Move back before the fire, just before the fire."

"Uh-huh." His breathing steadied again.

"Can you see a gun?"

"No."

"Can you see anybody in the car?"

"I see the driver's hands. And I see the top of the passenger's head. He's bending over. I see his hair. All I see is the top of his hair."

"What color hair?"

"I can't tell. It's too dark. I should have a flashlight."

"How long is the hair?"

"I can't tell. He's all in shadow."

"You see the driver's hands. What do they look like?"

"Small hands. Dark. She has a bracelet. It's silver-colored. That's what I see that's silver, the bracelet. The moonlight glances off it."

"Describe the bracelet."

"It's wide. It looks like a cuff."

"Like a handcuff?"

"Like a cuff on a sleeve. It's very wide. But it shines like a hand-cuff."

"Is there anything else you can see about the car or the people?"

"No. There's fire. I can't see past the fire." Without prompting, he had moved forward again to the moment of the shooting. "The fire is from the gun. He's shooting at me. I can't be shot; Cheryl's here. If I'm shot what will he do to her?"

"It's all right. Cheryl's all right. It's Sunday afternoon, Allen, all that is over with. Are you all right now?"

"No."

"What's wrong?"

"Jim thinks I did it. Jim thinks I killed a baby. I wouldn't kill a baby for anything."

"Nobody thinks you killed a baby," Neal assured him.

"No?"

"No. Honest, nobody thinks that. Go to sleep now, Allen," Neal said. "You'll sleep for five minutes, and then you'll wake and feel very rested and relaxed." Then, to McCain, he said, "Come out here in the hall and tell me what's going on."

Cheryl, feeling quite sure she already knew anything McCain was likely to say, didn't follow. She sat in the chair beside Allen's bed, and leaned forward to rest her head. She woke to Allen's hand very gently caressing her hair. "How long have I been asleep?" she asked drowsily.

"Couple of hours," he answered.

She sat up, suddenly feeling wide awake. "Oh my gosh! Did McCain leave?"

"Ages ago. He and Neal went off together."

"Oh, no! I have to talk to—where's the phone?"

"Slow down. What have you got to say to McCain that you haven't already said? You've had lots of time."

"When you were hypnotized, you said who drove the car."

"If I did, he'd have heard it too. But I don't think you're quite awake yet. Neal says I didn't add much of anything except a possible make on the vehicle."

"But there was one thing you did say," Cheryl answered. "You said the driver was a person with small dark hands who was wearing a very wide shiny silver bracelet that looked like a sleeve cuff. And I know who has a bracelet like that and would fit into this whole mess."

"Who, then?"

"Darling Corey. She has a wide silver bracelet with her initials on it that she wears all the time. And with her so dark, it looks even brighter on her than it would on most people." Allen looked puzzled, and Cheryl said, "Oh, don't you see? She's with—with whoever the mastermind of this deal is! He and Pitts were working together, and she was hiding Pitts, and we nearly walked in on them. So now he, whoever he is, has her hidden. And of course she was driving the car when you were ambushed because he couldn't drive and shoot at the same time. And furthermore," she added, "Darling Corey hasn't got a car, so the car must be his."

"Not necessarily," Allen answered. "They could have borrowed one just for the occasion, or they could have stolen one and ditched it. Or even, that late at night, they could have stolen one and returned it to the same spot, and unless the driver was really observant of his gasoline and his mileage he would quite possibly never even notice it had been used. But you're right, Cheryl, it does fit, and you do need to call McCain. Because if you're right, and it is Darling Corey, we've got to find her fast, because—think it through."

"He'll kill her next," Cheryl said slowly. "He has to kill her, sooner or later."

"Probably when he's about ready to leave. If he's sticking to the pattern he's set before, there'll be one or two post office robberies in the next couple of weeks. But he may not stick to the pattern because I wasn't in the pattern." Allen was silent for a moment. Then he added, "Cheryl, I know you have to go tell McCain about this. But I wish you'd stay with me for a little while longer first."

"I'd rather stay with you," Cheryl answered.

Allen was silent for a minute. Then he began speaking very rapidly, as if afraid he'd lose his nerve before the words came out. "I love you, Cheryl," he said. "I know you said you didn't want to be more than friends, but I love you so much I've got to say it. So please understand this. I know how you feel about—about the physical part of love. I'm not going to try to force anything on you you don't want, and I'm not asking you to love me. Just please—accept the fact that I love you because it makes me happy that I love you."

"You don't look very happy," Cheryl said. "Allen—" She dropped her head back down on the side of the bed. "I think I do love you, only I'm scared to death of love so I'm scared and I don't know what to do."

"You don't have to do anything." He turned over on his left side, balancing precariously with one knee drawn up and his cover very securely over his waist, and began stroking her hair again. "Just live from day to day, that's all, and I think one day you'll stop being scared. For now, just live from day to day and do what has to be done and don't worry about it."

"Only if you don't stop playing with my hair," she said in a muffled-sounding voice, "I'm never going to do what has to be done, which is for me to get up and go tell McCain about Darling Corey."

His hand, which had frozen into stillness at the first part of her sentence, began moving again, and his whole body shook with sudden laughter. "I would say, damn Darling Corey, but that's altogether too likely to come true. Do you like me to play with your hair?"

"Yes." Her voice still sounded muffled.

"Then I shall play with your hair on all possible occasions. Why do you like it?"

"I don't know. I just do."

"Then come back up here later and I'll play with your hair again. Right now I guess you have work to do."

"I guess I do." But she didn't move until Allen, at last and reluctantly, took his hands away and rolled over on his back. Then she sat up and looked at him accusingly. "Why did you stop?"

"Because you said you had work to do."

"It'll wait. He's not going to kill her today. I hope."

"Then unbraid your hair. Please, Cheryl?"

She unpinned the braids that crisscrossed on top of her head, took out the rubber-bands that anchored the braids, and pulled apart the braids. When she shook her head from side to side, her hair drifted free, below her shoulders, thick, straight, and very dark brown.

"Woman, you'll make a hair fetishist out of me yet," Allen said. "Why is your hair so beautiful?"

"Maybe because I'm a quarter Comanche."

"Are you really?" he asked delightedly. "I'm about an eighth Choctaw. But I think all I've gotten out of that, genetically, is being so darn short."

"That and the shape of your eyes. They're blue, but they're Choctaw shaped."

"Which side of your family is Comanche, or is it both?"

"My father's."

"Charlotte doesn't look Comanche at all."

"My real father—he died when I was a year old. It was my stepfather, Charlotte's father, who died when I was twelve. He adopted me, so I had his name and I always thought of him as my father. But he wasn't, really, and his family never did accept me much. That's why Charlotte has so many more cousins than I do."

"Oh?"

"Yeah. And she can't get it through her head that I wouldn't *have* them as cousins. Oh, like Waymon, that reporter she's dating now. He's about a third cousin on her daddy's side."

"I thought you were just meeting him the other day."

"I was. When he was a kid they didn't come around the house. Charlotte always went over there. That's why I was surprised to hear him introduced as her 'boyfriend.' He always used to pick on her when they were kids. Some of it was just funny, like chasing her with grass snakes, but some of it was plain mean and sneaky. She'd always come home crying when Dad had dragged her over there."

"Forget Charlotte," Allen said. "Did you ever meet any of your real father's family?"

"Not to remember," Cheryl answered. "Do you know any of your Choctaw relatives?"

"Oh, yes. I'm Choctaw on both sides. My parents were kind of distant cousins."

"Oh," Cheryl said and got a small hairbrush out of her purse and began to brush her hair.

"I would like watching you do that," Allen said, "except that I think it means you're fixing to put your hair out of my reach."

"I am," Cheryl said. "Also myself. I'm going to go tell McCain what we figured out. I am surpassed by nobody in my dislike for Darling Corey, but all the same I can't let her get murdered while we sit here and discuss my hair or our common racial heritage. Or our families."

"Promise to come back tonight?"

"If I can." Rapidly, without a mirror, she rebraided her hair and pinned it back on top of her head.

Allen sighed dramatically. "Oh, well," he said, "if you insist on going—"

"Which I do—"

"Then take care. Cheryl? I mean that. You know what kind of person you're after."

"I can look after myself."

"So can I, but I'm in the hospital all the same."

"I'll see you tonight, Allen," she said.

Cheryl had left her car in the hospital parking lot when she left with McCain; now she returned to it, finding it miserably hot. She turned on the air conditioner and was grateful for the braids, which kept the hair off her neck.

She was going to work because duty demanded she do so even though she was scheduled off, because she had spotted the clue in Allen's account that she knew McCain and the Ranger could not have spotted. She was not really too interested in keeping Darling Corey from being murdered; even her shock at the shooting of Allen and her disgusted anger at the murder of Lucille and her baby had receded into the back of her mind. She was, in fact, totally preoccupied with her own reactions to Allen's attention to her hair.

She knew she had beautiful hair. Men before Allen had wanted to play with it, but she'd always found the attention annoying, had in fact started braiding it partly as a defense mechanism, to keep people's hands away. But when Allen touched her head she wanted to unbraid her hair.

And that puzzled her; she couldn't understand why she should react that way. But she thought that perhaps she would be able to understand it if she let herself. That thought was frightening because she had been defending herself against involvement for so long. To go on and let this mean what it might mean would be to become defenseless; it would be to become vulnerable; it would be to become involved.

Perhaps she was already involved.

You've only been able to recognize him for five weeks, she scolded herself. You've really known him for less than one week. It's stupid to let go like this for someone you don't really know at all.

But, she thought as she walked into the police station, I wonder if I've ever really known anybody at all, because I know him better than I've ever known anybody else.

The air conditioning in the office was still out, and the building was unbelievably stuffy. Sergeant Hall, talking to six people at once, looked hot and uncomfortable. Glancing that way, Cheryl realized, first, that one of the six was Waymon; second, that all of them had pocket notebooks; and third, that four of them (including Waymon) had cameras. Reporters, she thought. But *six* of them? What are we doing with *six* of them?

Waymon glanced at her and punched another of the reporters. "Look," he said, "that's the officer I was telling you about, the one that's Charlotte's sister. She's the one that's working the Brantley killing. You'll want to talk to her."

"In the first place," Sergeant Hall said, "she is not working the Brantley killing. She did the initial work on it, but she is now extremely busy on another case. That one has been turned over to another officer. In the second place, Detective Burroughs has a direct order from me not to discuss this case or any other case with which she might happen to be involved with the press."

Eventually the other reporters left. Waymon showed some tendency to want to stay around and try to visit, but finally he, too, became discouraged enough to depart. "I appreciate that direct order; it'll save me a lot of trouble," Cheryl said, "but when did I get it?"

Sergeant Hall blinked. "Why, right then," he answered.

"Oh. I thought that might be it," Cheryl said. "Have McCain and Neal been in?"

"I haven't seen McCain in hours. Who's Neal?"

"Neal Ryan."

"Oh, that Neal. I was trying to think if there was a Neal who came with McCain. No, I haven't seen either one of them. Why?"

Cheryl recounted the hypnosis session, explaining, "But then I went to sleep, and they don't know that was Darling Corey he saw."

"You don't know that yourself."

"All right, no, I don't know it in the sense of being able to go into a courtroom and swear to it. But doesn't it sound like her to you, too?"

"I'll admit it does. And I was already upset because she was still missing. Not that I'd miss her if she got murdered," he emphasized, "it's just that I don't want another statistic here. We have enough statistics already."

Just then, Jim McCain charged in, followed by a man Cheryl hadn't seen before. "This is Richard Harvey," he announced. "Rick, this is Sergeant Hall and Detective Burroughs."

Rick Harvey looked younger than Cheryl. His sun-blond regulation-cut hair somehow managed to give an impression of unruly length. Tall, slim, and slightly swaybacked, he wore his belt just above the hips. Just now, he seemed slightly puzzled. "Hi," he said.

It was Cheryl who realized the cause of the puzzlement. "Hi, Rick," she said. "I'm Cheryl Burroughs, and he's Kenneth Hall. Welcome to the menagerie. Are you another postal inspector?"

"Sort of," he said. "I'm a document and fingerprint examiner in the lab in San Bruno, California."

Now it was Hall's turn to look puzzled. "We've already got lab people here from Memphis. Why San Bruno too?"

"No fingerprint people in Memphis," Rick explained. "Usually evidence comes to me, but this time, due to the situation, I've been invited to come to the evidence. I'll be fingerprinting all the checks that have been turning up forged."

"How is that going to help?" Sergeant Hall asked.

"It probably won't unless you can supply me fingerprint cards on every female arrested here in—say—the last three years. I hope you keep them?"

"Oh, yeah, we keep them. I'll get Skip to look them up." He went across the hall, returning moments later to add, "I've always said it's a shame we're too small to have fingerprint people of our own."

"Do you keep palm prints?" Rick asked.

"No. Should we?"

"I didn't expect you would. But it would be great if you did. You see, on checks we get palm prints more often than we do fingerprints. Especially the outside edge of the palm." Curling his hand into a writing position, he held it down on a desk top. "See?"

Hall turned his hands over, looking at them. "Oh," he said. "Yeah, I see that you would. Especially on the backs of the checks, right?"

"Right."

"Well, I'm sorry we don't have them. But nobody told me we ought to."

"Oh, well," Rick said, "it can't be helped. Is there a small room, like an interrogation room or something, but well lighted and ventilated, that I could set up as a temporary lab? I could use Conyers's office, but ninhydrin smells like the very devil and I'd hate to stink up the post office. It's easier to explain in a police station."

"I guess we could arrange a place," Hall said. "But what's ninhydrin?"

"It's a chemical we use to fingerprint checks. I like to use ninhydrin dissolved in ether because it doesn't make the ink run, but that's too explosive to use anywhere except in an absolutely static-free room. So we use ninhydrin dissolved in acetone. It's fairly safe, and most inks don't run in it."

"There's a former service station," Hall said, "that we once used as a police station before we got into this building. It's boarded up now, and we use it for storing recovered bicycles. It's as old as the seven hills, but the office area is well lighted, and the shop area is well ventilated. Will that do?"

"It sounds fine," Rick said, "except for the bicycles."

"Oh, well, we'll get a couple of run-arounds to move them this afternoon," Hall said. "Now, Skip is finding those cards, but would it help any if we rounded up all the whores and got new sets of fingerprints and palm prints?"

"You can't do that," McCain answered, aghast.

"Why can't I?"

"Because there's no probable cause."

"Sure there is," Hall interrupted. "If the chief orders this force to crack down on prostitution for a few days, it's certainly none of the post office's business. Now, is it?"

"Not if you make a legal arrest on a real case and follow through on the prostitution charge," McCain said. "But take it easy, will you? When we get this killer, I want to nail his ass to the wall; I don't want him getting out on any damn technicality."

"They'll be good arrests," Hall promised and took off toward the chief's office.

"Jim," Cheryl said, "when I finally woke up this afternoon—"

"When was that? I figured you were really worn out."

"I was," she said. "But listen. I shouldn't have gone to sleep. I needed to talk to you because I recognized one of the descriptions Allen gave."

"What are you talking about? He described one person's hands and the top of another person's head, and even those weren't any kind of real descriptions."

"Not to make sense to you," she agreed. "But I'm about sure I know who was wearing the bracelet."

"Who, then?"

"Darling Corey. She has a bracelet just like that, and I've never seen her without it except when she was in jail."

McCain slammed his left fist into his right palm. "Damn!" he almost shouted. "That fits. That does fit! Goddamn, why can't we find that bitch?"

"Because she's holed up with the killer," Cheryl answered. "She's got to be. That's the only answer that makes sense."

"Then now's when I crap in your mess kit again," McCain said, unusually coarse. "There's one man in this town who, from all appearances, has enough influence on the whores to pull this caper off, and we know he can organize, and we know he knows about evidence. And he's not at home right now. You said he was in Shreveport. Well, he's not in Shreveport unless he's staying with somebody; the police there checked every motel they've got, from the Hilton on down to the rattiest flea trap. And he's not there. Only he was there—he was in Shreveport—the day a man was shot to death in a post office in Bossier City with the same gun your boyfriend was shot with."

Cheryl didn't protest this time at hearing Allen described as her boyfriend. She answered very quietly, "It's not John. I know that. It's not John."

"Then who the hell is it, Cheryl? And where the hell is Darling Corey Wilson?"

***

• 106 •

Darling Corey was dancing quietly, all by herself, on a carpeted floor. She had a drink and a cigarette in one hand; the cigarette wasn't tobacco, and it was laced with little white crystals of cocaine. She was humming along with the record; she was happy.

"You likin' it, baby?" the man asked, sitting in his big recliner chair watching Darling Corey dance.

"I likin' it," Darling Corey answered somnolently.

"You still think I'm stupid?"

"You ain't stupid. You bees the Man."

"Do a strip tease for me, baby."

Darling Corey laughed lightly and put her dripping glass down on top of the wood cabinet of the stereo. She put her cigarette in the ash tray, careful to snuff it out all the way. Laughing, still dancing, she stripped off her blouse and tossed it to the man, who was watching intently. She went on dancing; the beat of the music was almost as intoxicating as the glass and the cigarette. She reached around to unhook the bra, and pitched it to him. He dropped the blouse and the bra on the floor. The dark tips of her nipples were firm as she went on dancing.

The man sat quite still, watching Darling Corey dance. When she was completely nude, he got up and began to unfasten his belt. . . . Ten minutes later he stood up. "I got to go," he told her. "I'll be back later. You be here."

"But you just came," she protested. "You can't go now, man; I ain't even through yet."

"That's right," he said, "I just came. And now I'm going. You stay here, you understand?"

"And what if I don't?" she pouted.

In one motion, he had a switchblade out of his pocket and open. "You want to wind up like Lucille?"

"Oh, no!" She cowered back, covering her breasts, the silver bracelet that was the only thing she wore gleaming brightly.

"Then you be here when I get back."

He left, slamming the door, and Darling Corey heard him driving down the street. After a while, she went to sleep.

Much later, she got up. Not bothering to dress, she turned the record over, relit the cigarette, and poured a little more whiskey into the glass. She didn't bother with any more ice.

She didn't like having to stay inside. It was too much like being in jail. But if she had to stay inside, this was a damn good place to do it. They don't, she reminded herself, treat you like this in jail.

Darling Corey danced, nude but for the streak of silver, alone in the twilight.

·Seven·

Saturday and Sunday Cheryl had worked on her own time and could follow her own schedule. But Monday found her somewhat depressed, parking her car at 7:30 beside the old building that had once served as the Lakeport Police Station before the formation of the county department. Mondays were usually rotten days, but this one, she expected, would be worse than usual.

The heavily metallic acrid smell that must be ninhydrin hung heavy in the still air; Rick Harvey was already working. He had the overhead doors to the old service bays open; inside, he had strung twine wall to wall. He had rows of treasury checks, pink or green or grey, attached to the twine with wooden clothes pins. He was vigorously spraying them with something from a white pressure can.

He came outside, pulling off the little painter's mask he'd been wearing. "Whew!" he said, wiping his face with his forearm. "That stuff gets to you fast! And I didn't think to ask last night whether the damn place had an air conditioner. I'm going to have to try to round up a window unit."

"Why are your hands purple?" Cheryl asked.

"That's the ninhydrin. It works on the amino acids the perspiration from people's hands leaves on checks. Unfortunately, it also works on the amino acids in my perspiration, so whenever I don't wear gloves, I run around with purple hands. And the fact is, I hate to work in gloves." He looked back at the building. "One thing about it, with that place as hot and humid as it is, the prints ought to develop fast."

"Good," Cheryl said. "But I really don't see how you're going to be able to use any prints you do get if you don't have any suspects' prints to compare them with."

"Non-suspect idents are more fun anyway," Rick said casually. "Almost all the checks have been cashed by young women, apparently under twenty-five and possibly all prostitutes. Therefore, I have the fingerprint cards of all the women under thirty who've been arrested here lately to compare them with. There aren't many, but they'll be a start. After that, I'll decide what to do next.''

"I can see that that would take a while," Cheryl said, wondering how anybody could make sense of fingerprints.

"Just a few days," Rick said. "Hey, do me a favor. Tell Allen I'll come by and see him when I get a chance. Is he doing okay?"

"Well, considering the circumstances—" Cheryl said.

"Yeah," Rick said. "Considering the circumstances. *Damn* the circumstances," he added violently. "We've got to stop that son of a bitch."

Cheryl went on into the police station, where Sergeant Hall hung up the phone and looked at her. "I was just trying to call you," he said. "You've been working your tail off all weekend, and I'm about ninety-five percent sure I'm going to need you to work late tonight. Why don't you take off this morning? Go see Allen, or go home and get some sleep or something."

"Okay," Cheryl said. She'd rather go see Allen later and work earlier, but she'd rather go see Allen early than not at all that day.

He was sitting up, with the head of the bed turned up for him to lean on. The radio was set to a country and western station which, ironically, was playing "Darling Corey." He clearly didn't see Cheryl come in; he was drinking ice water and reading. "Hi, Allen," she said.

He looked at her and grinned. "Thanks for looking after me," he said. "May I assume the Snoopy radio belongs to Holly?"

"Yes, but she doesn't need it right now. I dropped it by for you last night."

"I appreciate it. What's new at the police station?"

"We've acquired, for the moment, one Rick Harvey. He says he'll come see you when he's got time."

The grin widened. "Good. I like Rick. He helped me out a lot last year on a check case."

"And McCain now thinks John Arnold is it."

The grin faded. "I can see why he thinks so."

"You don't, do you, Allen?"

"If he wasn't vouched for by you," Allen said slowly, "I'd be looking at him very hard right now. As it is, I respect your opinion. But even so, I'll admit it has crossed my mind that although you know his family, you haven't really known him for long."

"Maybe not," Cheryl said. "But Allen, I know something factual that would rule him out even if I didn't know his character."

"What is it, then? Let me rule him out too if I can."

"He always uses a .45," Cheryl said. "He was in the military for so long, and he learned to shoot with a .45. He despises a .32; he calls it a popgun. He says if somebody shot him with one and he found out about it, he'd disarm the person and spank him."

"Ha," Allen said. "Have I got news for him."

"I know. He was just talking, of course. But the other thing is, he's a dead shot. If he'd shot you, he wouldn't have hit you where you were hit."

"Meaning, I wouldn't be around to cry on your shoulder and make a general nuisance of myself."

"Meaning, you wouldn't be around to play with my hair and be rude to yourself."

"I'm never rude to myself. All right, Cheryl, if it isn't John, and I think even McCain has ruled me out, where do we look now?"

"It's somebody who doesn't live here," Cheryl said. "Because if he hit first in Hopewell Springs, and then in Bossier City, and now here, he can't live in all three places, so chances are he doesn't live in any one of them."

"Unless he moves around a lot like a construction worker or something like that. And I'll admit he doesn't sound like a construction worker to me." He drank some more ice water. "Somebody who gets around," he said. "Maybe like a gypsy trucker."

"What's a gypsy trucker?"

"Know what a tramp steamer is?"

"One that goes to one port, unloads, and then hangs around there until it finds another cargo."

"Well, a gypsy trucker is the same thing, only he's got eighteen wheels instead of a steam engine. What else? A bush pilot? He could be all over the place and nobody would ever notice he was gone. What else?"

"A millionaire playboy. A jet setter."

"Do we know any of those?"

"Nope."

"Aren't you supposed to be at work?" Allen asked. "Not that I want to run you off, but I wouldn't want Hall to, either."

"I am at work, see?" She pointed to the walkie-talkie she'd set on the table. "No, I'm probably going to have to work tonight, so Hall told me to take off this morning. Anyway, I worked all weekend when I was scheduled off. Is there anything I can go get for you today while I've got time?"

"Have you still got my keys?"

"Yes."

"Then will you please go by my apartment and get me a decent bathrobe?" he said. "I'm supposed to be out walking up and down the hall, getting exercise or some such matter, and that garment they expect me to wear is not decent."

"Do you have a new bathrobe?"

"Not very." He thought about it. "In fact, I have a very *un*new bathrobe. I think I got it seven years ago."

"What size do you wear?"

"Cheryl, you can't—"

"Oh yes I can. If you don't tell me I'll just go look in the old one and find out."

"Medium, I guess. I can't even remember how the things are sized."

She decided to go first to his apartment, to be sure medium was really the right size. Gosh, she decided on arrival, this would be a dismal place for an injured man to have to come home to. She stripped the bed, leaving it to air, and bundled the sheets and what dirty clothes she could find to take them home and wash them. She put the dishes in the sink to soak, took in Saturday's mail (but threw it away when she found it consisted only of circulars), and got rid of the accumulation of newspapers. There was no use, she thought, in dusting now; she'd do that when he was ready to go home. Only then did she hunt for a bathrobe size and, on further consideration, a shoe size.

She went to Ward's and found him a decent bathrobe and a pair of slippers and went back to take them to him. One good thing about being a cop, she thought, you don't have to wait for visiting hours.

He was asleep; the book had slipped from his hand. She put a sheet of paper in it as a bookmark, closed it, and set it beside him. Then she slipped back out, leaving the robe and slippers by his bed.

Half the morning spent. She felt like going back to work, but reminded herself that Hall had told her to take the morning off. It seemed rather a waste of time, wandering about being domestic when the person who shot Allen and butchered Lucille Brantley was still at large.

If Holly had been home she could have spent the morning enjoyably, even usefully. But Holly wasn't home, and there was no use visiting her at her father's house. That would just upset them both.

She went back home and put Allen's sheets, and her own too, into the washer. On consideration, she thought it might be a good idea to straighten her own somewhat neglected house while the machine was running. Then she put the laundry into the dryer and put a load of her own clothes (and some of Allen's) in to wash. While she waited for them, she reread some of Allen's notes, but they didn't make her think of anything else that could point to the killer.

She folded Allen's sheets and put her own back on the bed, and threw the load of clothes into the dryer. Eleven-thirty. That would be about half a day. She made a peanut butter sandwich and turned on the television to watch the noon news.

Then she got the clothes out of the dryer and put them all on hangers, pleased to find Allen's shirts were wash and wear and somewhat annoyed at the one blouse she always had to iron. She certainly wasn't going to iron it now.

Twelve o'clock. Surely that counted as half a day off. She drove to the police station.

The four Lakeport detectives inside appeared thoroughly outnumbered by five postal inspectors, three postal laboratory men, and an FBI agent; and the thirteen law enforcement people—fourteen counting Cheryl—were outnumbered by the reporters. Sergeant Hall was saying, "That's all we can say right now."

"Inspector McCain!" one of the reporters shouted.

"That's all we can say right now," McCain confirmed. "When we know any more, we'll tell you."

"What is the present condition of Inspector Conyers?"

"He's in very good condition," McCain said.

"Is it true that he's engaged to a policewoman on this department?"

That had to have originally come from Waymon, and Cheryl wanted to crawl through the floor. She was glad to be at the back of the room, unnoticed by the reporters, and grateful to hear Hall reply, "No, that is not true. Look, we've told you all we can. I don't understand why you're suddenly making such a big fuss over this. I'll ask you to clear on out now."

"Is it true that a reward is being offered?"

McCain stood up and cleared his throat. "Let me give you a complete answer on that," he said rather loudly. Two television news-people, spotting something usable, turned on video tape recorders. McCain continued, "A reward of $10,000 has been offered for information leading to the arrest and conviction of the person or persons responsible for the murder of Inspector Matthew Elton in Bossier City, Louisiana, last October. We feel fairly certain at this point that the same person who murdered him is also the person who assaulted Inspector Conyers and murdered Ms. Brantley; however, at this time, no decision has been made to offer a reward in the matter of the shooting of Inspector Conyers and, of course, there is no federal jurisdiction in the Brantley killing."

He divided his attention between the two video cameras as he continued, "At this time, the murder of Ms. Brantley is still under considerable investigation, and few facts in it have been determined. However, we do know for certain that a second person was present when Inspector Conyers was shot. That person was driving the vehicle used in the assault. We are fairly sure we know who that person is. I have been authorized by the U. S. Attorney for this district to promise that person immunity from prosecution if that person will agree to testify against the assailant. Of course, if that assailant should, as we expect, turn out also to be Inspector Elton's murderer, that person would then become eligible for the $10,000 reward."

As reporters scattered to try to catch deadlines, racing one another for the few downtown pay phones, Sergeant Hall said somberly, "You've either made Darling Corey rich or signed her death warrant. And I'm afraid it's going to be the latter. I wish you hadn't done that."

Jim McCain got out his cigarettes and lighter and carefully lit a cigarette before answering. "She's disposable," he said. "I'd rather have her alive, as a witness, but she's disposable if it'll bring Mr. Big out of the woodwork to have her dead."

"It might drive him farther back in," Cheryl pointed out. "Anyway, what right do *you* have to say she's disposable? You never even saw her."

"We've got to catch this bastard," McCain said defensively. "You don't think she's disposable? I think she's a hell of a lot more disposable than postal inspectors."

"I agree with that," Cheryl said, "but what I'm trying to say is that it might get her killed without doing any good at all. It might just drive him farther into the woodwork or even out of town completely."

"It might," McCain agreed, shortly. "I took the chance." He put out his cigarette and instantly lit another.

Into the silence came Rick Harvey's voice. "Would anybody like to go arrest Dovie Ledbetter?" he asked. "I've been dying to ask, but I couldn't until the hounds had departed."

"Exactly what are we arresting her for?" Hall inquired. "I mean, I assume the gist of it, but to get a warrant it would help to know the particulars."

"She seems to have cashed this check," Rick Harvey said, carefully nonchalant. He produced the check, once again packaged in a plastic sleeve to protect the newly-developed fingerprints from contamination. "At least she's handled it a lot. Let's see—it's an income tax refund check, number—oh, well, you can copy that from the check—made out to Carolyn Jamison for three hundred and seventy-two dollars. And it's got Dovie's fingerprints all over it. Who's going to take the warrant?"

"I can," McCain began.

But Hall interrupted, "I'll bet I can get a state warrant faster than you can get a federal warrant."

"Yeah, get the state warrant," McCain said. "And I'll get authorization to hold her in protective custody so that she can't make bond."

Cheryl wanted to go out and help arrest Dovie Ledbetter. But no matter what the major crime may be in a city, the other things continue, too. Detectives had already scattered when another call came in. Cheryl found herself sent to work a reported mugging while Hall went with McCain to pick up Dovie. It turned out not to be a mugging at all; it was a theft, and not even an interesting theft. In fact, it was the kind of theft that had frequently made Cheryl think that if she were the victim she wouldn't have the nerve to report it.

Miss Minnie Jordan had left a twenty-dollar bill in her purse on the seat of her car when she went into the nursery to pick up her little brother. When she got back, the purse was on the ground beside the car, and the money was gone.

Well, no, the car wasn't locked. But why should she lock it, she demanded. She was just going to be gone for a minute, and just into the nursery, for heaven's sake.

Cheryl went back to the station feeling thoroughly frustrated, to find Dovie Ledbetter, who at two hundred and eighty pounds should have been fairly easily identifiable even to the most forgetful forgery victim, weeping with her head on Lloyd Methvin's desk. Dovie wept loudly. Her curly red hair clung damply to her head, her china-blue eyes reddened, her translucent porcelain skin roughened, her nose ran, and all four of her chins quivered as she wept. McCain looked as frustrated and as disgusted as Cheryl felt.

"You cain't arrest me," Dovie wailed. "If the Man thinks I talked he'll kill me for sure!"

"You'll be in jail," Hall pointed out. "He can't get at you in jail."

"Look, Dovie," McCain said, "that's what protective custody means. It means we've got you locked up so he can't get at you. After we've got him in jail, we can let you back out if you cooperate with us."

"He'll get at me in jail," Dovie said. "He'll get me anyway."

"If you'll tell us who he is, we'll go and arrest him," McCain said. "Then he'll be in jail and you can go home. But if we just turn around and let you go now, right after arresting you, then he'll think for sure you told us something."

"I tell you he'll kill me," Dovie sobbed. "He killed Lucille. You know how he killed Lucille?" Dovie clearly knew. "He took pitchers," she said. "He took pitchers while he was killing Lucille. I seen them. He kills everybody gets in his way. I cain't tell you—" She broke down in another storm of weeping.

You can talk with stubborn witnesses. You can talk with disagreeable witnesses. You can talk with reluctant witnesses. But there's not much you can do with terrified witnesses.

They put Dovie in jail, assuring her again that nobody could get at her there.

Just after she was led out, Rudy Garcia came into the detective bureau, teeth flashing startlingly white in his dark face as he grinned. "Did I hear somebody was looking for Mary Jane Rowe?" he asked.

McCain turned. "Yeah," he said. "She's a possible witness. Maybe even a possible suspect. Did you find her?"

"Yeah," Garcia said, "I found her."

"Well?"

"Well, what?" Garcia was an even-tempered, competent, and methodical man. But he didn't like undue haste. His way of dealing with McCain's hurry was to become, perhaps unconsciously, slower and slower, with the result that McCain spoke even faster.

"Did you bring her in?"

Garcia scratched his chin with his thumb. Cheryl, who knew him well, was sure by now that he was deliberately being annoying. "No," he said.

"Why?" McCain, who didn't know Garcia, demanded.

"Nobody told me to bring her in," Garcia said. "They just told us in muster that if anybody saw her you were to be notified."

"Then will you please notify me!" Garcia said. "Where was she, and what was she doing?"

The game abruptly abandoned, Garcia spoke crisply. "She was sweeping the Reverend Elijah Miller's Gospel Tabernacle. She told me she has Done Been Saved and now she cooks in Reverend Elijah Miller's lunchroom. You want her? I'll go get her, but I'll tell you beforehand, I asked Reverend 'Lijah and he said she's been sleeping in a back room there and hasn't been off the place in three months except to go shopping. And before you ask, Reverend 'Lijah's not as hinky as he sounds."

McCain looked at Hall, who answered. "As the man says, Reverend 'Lijah's not as hinky as he sounds."

"Well, I'll go talk to her anyway," McCain said.

The fruitless visit left McCain even more frustrated. Shorn of Biblical commentary, what Mary Jane had to say was that she had not seen either Darling Corey Wilson or Lucille Brantley in months, had no idea what they had been doing, and wasn't at all interested in finding out. And now if she could be excused, she had beans cooking.

"Damn!" McCain said outside. He slammed the car door hard, started the car, jerked into reverse, and struck a short post outlining the parking area. "Damn!" he said again. He got out of the car, examined the post and the rear bumper, determined there was no damage to either, jerked the gear into forward, and took off. Cheryl said something under her breath about gear jamming. McCain waited until he got to a stoplight before he glared at her.

Allen would see the humor in it, she thought. But this man doesn't.

As McCain said he had to confer with Hall again, they went back to the police station. There, Cheryl, expecting to have to go back out again with McCain after the conference, sat at her desk impatiently reading case reports. The telephone rang again, and she and Hall grabbed it at the same time.

"We got a call to a child abuse," the dispatcher said. "Uniform man at the scene says he thinks he better have a detective."

"Okay," Hall said, "Just a minute." He covered the mouthpiece. "Cheryl, you better go. There's just you and Lloyd available."

"Okay," Cheryl said, thinking she would rather work a child abuse than go back out with McCain this afternoon. "What's the address?"

"2142 Linda," the dispatcher said.

"Oh, my God, that's Holly!" Cheryl cried. She dropped the phone and reached for car keys.

Hall grabbed her arm. "That's what?" he demanded.

"That's Holly! She's with Terry this month. 2142 Linda, that's where Terry lives. Please let go of me!"

"I'll let go of you, but I'm driving."

In the car, Cheryl asked, "Who called?"

"A neighbor. Said the child had been crying for hours. It may not be so bad, Cheryl. She may just be cross or upset about being away from home."

"Then why did the uniform man call for a detective? Anyway, you don't know Terry. He'll have been drinking. He's okay when he doesn't drink." She took her jacket off, removed her shoulder holster, and put her jacket back on. "I don't think I'd better go in with this on," she said with rather numb logic, putting the gun in the glove box.

Holly was still crying when they arrived. "Mama!" she screamed and ran to Cheryl's arms. "Please let's go home! Mama, I don't want to stay here, please tell Mr. Judge Dors I want to go home!"

"It's okay, baby, I'll take you home," Cheryl promised, rocking Holly in her arms and trying to find a place to sit down. The patrolman stood over a sullen Terry glowering in the corner. Hall knocked a pornographic paperback, a beer can, a shoe, and a belt off the couch to make room for Cheryl and the child. When the crying finally stopped, Cheryl said, "Sit up, now, Holly, and let Mama see."

Holly had a black eye. Her right cheek was bruised, and there was a cut on her lip. Her pink house mouse shirt, that Cheryl had washed for her a week ago, was stained with blood and on her wrong side out over her Wonder Woman underwear. She was wearing the pink shorts that went with the house mouse shirt, but she had them on backwards. Her hair was tangled and seemed to have jelly in it.

"Alton," Cheryl said to the patrolman, "Holly has a few clothes and toys here. Would you please see if you can find them? I think she'd like to pack them up and go home."

"I've walked through the house," Alton said. "She doesn't need anything that's here. I'm sorry, Cheryl." The glance he threw Terry wasn't a friendly one. "I already gave him his rights," he added. "He had his hands on her throat when I came in the door. I could see it from the street."

"What did he do, Holly?" Cheryl asked.

"He said—he said he had an awful head on him," Holly said, still with an occasional sob. "And I said it didn't look any awfuler than usual. So he hitted me, and I cried. And he threw my dolly on the floor and broke her. And he kept telling me to shut up. And I couldn't shut up because he hitted me and hitted me. And he hitted me last night because I said I was hungry, and he said I was too rotten to feed. And he already had been gone all day and didn't take me at the nursery and then he went away again at night and the peanut butter is all gone."

Alton went back to the kitchen and came back with a Coke. "Here, honey," he said.

"I'm not allowed a Coke," Holly said. "Because it has too much sugar an' caffeine. Mama said so."

"You can have it today anyhow," Cheryl said, "to hold you until you get something to eat."

"Oh," Holly said, "thank you." She reached for the Coke.

"I'll get you some crackers as soon as we get to the police station," Cheryl added.

Terry hiccuped and stood up. "Get the bitches outta my house," he said.

"Up against the wall," Alton said. "We're getting *you* out of the house right now. You're under arrest for aggravated assault." He patted Terry down, removed a buck knife from his pocket, and began to handcuff him.

Hall picked the knife up and looked at it. "Over legal length," he said. "That's real nice. What do you use it on, little girls?"

"That's my fish-cleaning knife," Terry protested, struggling against the handcuffs. "And I wasn't hurting Holly. I *love* Holly. I was jus' spanking her a little."

"Uh-huh," Sergeant Hall said, looking at Holly. "Sure you were. Cheryl, didn't you tell me you have a petition in court to terminate Terry's parental rights?"

"Yes," she said bitterly, "but Judge Dors keeps postponing it." She glanced after Terry, who was being led out, and a sense of justice made her add, "This never happened before. It was just because I didn't want him around her."

"It may never have happened before," he answered, "but if she keeps coming over here it'll happen again. Take Holly up to Judge Dors right now. Friend of Terry's or not, I think he'll get the point."

Cheryl didn't even stop long enough to wash Holly's face, although she did insist on clean hands before Holly ate the peanut-butter crackers out of the machine at the station. She appeared at Judge Dors's office, and Martine, the judge's secretary, looked up in astonishment. "Cheryl, what's wrong with that child?" she asked.

"I'd like to talk to Judge Dors about what's wrong with this child," Cheryl answered. "Holly, can you sit here with Miss Young while I talk with the judge?"

A few moments later, Judge Dors came into the front office. "Holly," he asked, "do you want Terry Rhoads to be your daddy?"

"No!" Holly said.

"Why?"

"He's mean to me. I hate to go there. He hits me and he doesn't like to give me supper except hamburgers and peanut butter. And one day he went away and didn't take me at the nursery and didn't come back until at night, and noises came in the house. And he made me ride in his airplane and he flied it upside down and I threw up and he hitted me. Then the next time he flied in his airplane he didn't take me and he didn't go home until at night again, and then he brought a lady with him and she laughed at me and said I was a poor baby. I'm not a baby. I'm five. Mama told me I had to go visit him four weeks because Mr. Judge Dors said so. Are you Mr. Judge Dors?"

"Yes, Holly, I'm Judge Dors."

"Please don't make me go there any more." She started to cry again. "Please, I want to go home with my mama."

Judge Dors looked over at Cheryl. "You need to realize," he said, "that every time I've talked with him he assured me he really cared about her, and that there was just a personality conflict between you and him. I had no reason to doubt him. It's a common enough situation."

"He does care about her," Cheryl said, "when he doesn't have to take any kind of responsibility for her. He goes out to my mother's house when Holly's out there and visits—takes her toys, that sort of thing. He just can't stand any sort of crimp in his life-style."

"Some people can't," the judge said. "Men or women, it doesn't matter. Martine, find me the file, and write out an order. In the case of Cheryl Burroughs vs. Terry Rhoads, in the interests of Holly Burroughs, a minor, parental rights of Terry Rhoads are hereby terminated. He will retain visitation rights only if visits are conducted in the presence of her mother or grandmother."

"What does that mean?" Holly demanded.

"It means he's not your daddy anymore," Cheryl said, "but he can visit you at Granny's house if you want him to."

"But I don't have to go stay at his house any more?"

"Not ever again. I'll take you home now, and we'll get you a bath and some clean clothes. And you can tell me what you want for supper."

"Green beans?"

"Green beans and what else?"

"Can I have macaroni and cheese? And can I have a Popsicle or some ice cream?"

"Macaroni and cheese and ice cream and green beans," Cheryl said. "Just as soon as I can get home and make supper." But she had to go back to the detective bureau first. "Sergeant," she said. "whatever was on for tonight, can you reset it?"

"Jim and I were just talking about that," Hall answered. "We were going to try to round up some whores for fingerprints, but since we've got one in jail now, we decided to hold off on that. And you aren't on call tonight unless it's something to do with this case."

With the macaroni cooking and Holly in the bathtub, Cheryl called Allen. It was the first time she'd ever heard him do any serious swearing. Then he asked, "Were you calling to tell me you can't come this evening?"

"I'm sorry," she said, "but Holly's got to come first."

"Of course she does," he agreed, "but I was thinking it would be great if you'd come on and bring her. I wouldn't want her to go through like thinking the world is made up of men like—like him."

"You know children under ten aren't allowed past the lobby."

"But I could meet you in the lobby. I've been walking around a lot today."

"I'm afraid she'd try to climb on you."

"Explain to her why she can't. Then, if she forgets, I'll explain again."

"And she'd want to ask you ten million questions."

"Then I'll answer ten million questions. Please, Cheryl? I think she and I would be good for each other. And let her ask the questions. I don't care if they're personal ones."

Cheryl thought, suddenly, that if there'd been someone like Allen around when she was a child, things might have been better for her. "Okay," she capitulated, "I'll be there about seven-thirty."

Allen cornered the next Candystriper he saw and asked her to go to the gift shop and find something for a five-year-old. When she returned with a red plastic fire truck, he stared at it in some dismay. "I forgot to say a five-year-old girl."

"That's all right," the Candystriper said. "She'll like it."

"Are you sure?"

"Sure I'm sure. I'm a girl. And nobody ever gave me a toy fire truck. I always wanted one."

Dovie, looking out the barred windows, froze in sudden terror. Was that the Man walking by? Yes, it was, and he was looking up at the windows of the jail. Had he seen her?

She stepped back from the window as fast as she could, but he paused for a moment, looking up. He'd seen her.

She set to work with feverish anxiety. He wouldn't get her. No, he wouldn't get her, not to chop her up the way he chopped up Lucille.

But he might be coming here . . . She had to hurry. . . .

"Holly, please be a quiet fire truck," Cheryl said. "There are sick people here, and I'm sure they don't want to hear you be a siren."

"But I never saw a quiet fire truck," Holly protested.

"Then you be one, and you'll have invented something new."

"Just imagine," Allen added, "that you are sneaking up on the fire, very quietly, so it doesn't hear you and run away."

Holly put the fire truck down and came over to lean her elbows on

Allen's knees and look up at him. "Mama says I can't crawl all over you because your tummy hurts because you got shot."

"That's right."

"Did it hurt real bad?"

"It sure did."

"Did you cry?" Holly asked. "I cried when my daddy that isn't my daddy any more hitted me."

"I don't remember if I cried or not," he said. "But I know I threw up. That was yucky because I couldn't get up and so I threw up all over myself. Did you ever do that?"

"Oh, yeah," Holly agreed eagerly. "I did that when my daddy flied upside down. But one time last year I threw up, and Mama washed me and she got me a trash can so I could throw up in it if I wanted to throw up again, but I threw up on my bed instead, and Mama said she'd rather work a homicide than clean up after me again. Did she tell you that?"

"No, she didn't tell me that," Allen said. "I don't think she wanted to work a homicide right then." It appeared to Cheryl that he was trying very hard not to laugh, which didn't seem to make too much sense.

"Oh," Holly said and returned to being a fire truck.

"What's going on in the real world?" Allen asked Cheryl, and she told him about Dovie, and about Mary Jane, and about the reward speech McCain had made. "He shouldn't have done that," Allen said. "Damn, I don't like that. And I know he knows better." Then, frowning, he asked, "And Dovie's white?"

"Yeah," Cheryl said and giggled abruptly. "Allen, can you imagine anybody paying to go to bed with something like that?"

"Uh-uh," Allen said. "But I thought all the check passers were black."

"No."

"Then that's another factor to think about," Allen said. "And it's one I don't think McCain's really thought about."

"I don't think McCain thinks about much of anything except his ego," Cheryl answered. "Oh, that's not fair, is it? But did I tell you—"

An hour later, Allen had to say, "Cheryl, I'm sorry, I'm about to give out."

"You want me to call a nurse?"

"No, I'll make it back upstairs. Thanks for coming and for bringing Holly."

"Did you call me?" Holly asked, looking up from a close examination of the underside of her fire truck.

"I have to go to bed now," Allen said.

"Is it past your bedtime?"

"Yeah, I'm afraid it is. But I want to thank you for coming to visit me."

"I hope you feel better," she said.

Allen was shaking with exhaustion by the time he made it back to bed. But despite a nagging worry about the safety of Darling Corey and of the unknown-to-him Dovie, he felt happy; he felt relaxed. Almost, he even felt comfortable, except for that unending pain that, right now, was so close to being bearable that he could almost ignore it. Thinking about Cheryl, he slid into sleep, and the nurse who came to give him a sleeping pill didn't even wake him; she only made a note to check on him in case he woke later and needed medication.

But Cheryl was not asleep, and Holly was not at home. Holly was at her grandmother's house, asleep in Charlotte's bed, and Cheryl was working the suicide in the jail.

And Terry was already out on bond.

·Eight·

*A*llen woke at nine-forty-five, ravenously hungry and convinced, at least emotionally, that he could go out and start jogging. Logic assured him that by the time he had walked to the end of the hall he'd be exhausted, but the hunger was another matter. He made up his mind that if he could not persuade the doctor to allow him solid food he was going to see what Cheryl would smuggle in; or, failing that, he'd gather up what change he had and search the hospital for a cracker machine. After all, he'd been on a liquid diet since Saturday, and as supper Friday night didn't count, because he'd lost it, the last real meal he'd had was lunch Friday. And it was now what, Tuesday? Yes, Tuesday. And the more he thought about being hungry, the hungrier he felt.

He wondered what time it was. When he picked up his watch from the table beside the bed, he wondered why he had been allowed to sleep so late, instead of, as usual, being awakened at six-thirty. He climbed out of bed. He'd been allowed only sponge baths, but he knew there was a shower in the room. The hell with not getting the bandage wet, he thought, they can always change the bandage. He had a shower and then brushed his teeth and shaved standing up instead of fussing with that little hand basin they kept insisting on his using.

By then he expected to start being tired, but he wasn't too tired, and he wasn't even hurting very much.

Somebody had come and changed his bed while he was in the shower. Maybe they weren't going to fuss about the shower.

He didn't want to lie down again. So he grabbed the book he'd been reading and got a glass of ice water, which he didn't expect was going to make him feel any less hungry, and sat down. Then he got up again and pulled the chair over by the window.

Then he decided he didn't want to read. He was tired of reading. He got the folder containing his notes out from under the bedside table and opened it to leaf through the notes again. But he'd been through them too many times already. They all wound up in little cues to himself to see this person, ask that question. And probably somebody else had already seen all those people, asked all those questions. He wanted to be able to go back to work.

The door opened, and Dr. Boyd came in. "I dropped by early this morning because I had to be in surgery at seven. You looked to be sleeping so well I told the nurses just to let you sleep. How are you feeling?"

"Great," Allen said. "When can I go back to eating?"

"Not today, anyhow, I'm afraid."

"Oh, hell," Allen said in dismay. "I wasn't hungry until today, so I didn't really care, but—"

"But now you're hungry. Allen, I'm sorry. I'd like to be able to tell you to go on and eat whatever you want to. But you're just going to have to stick with liquids for at least a couple more days. Right now I expect that Thursday evening you can start on something light, but there's just too much risk in doing it right now."

"Risk of what? It's my risk, anyway."

"Risk of peritonitis, which could kill you, and risk of causing some complications that could result in you having to run around the rest of your life with a little plastic bag taped to your side, which you're damn lucky you don't have right now." Dr. Boyd decided to sit down. "And as to it being your risk, it seems to me you've got somebody else involved in your life now. Which makes it no longer just your risk. Or am I speaking out of turn?"

Allen hesitated before answering. "No. Not really." He stared at the wall. "I'm just a little disappointed."

"You mind if I talk to you like I would to my brother if he were in your shoes?"

"No. Go ahead."

"You're a gutsy man. You've been turning down pain medication almost constantly since you got into this hospital, and whether you happen to believe me or not, I do know exactly what you've been going through. You expect a lot of yourself, and one of the things you expect is to be able to heal like you were half the age you are. Well, I've got news for you. You are healing like a man half your age. But it's still not going to be an overnight thing."

"Okay," Allen said.

"And I'll tell you something else. Conservative medical practice would have put one of those little plastic bags on you, at least for a while. I decided to take a calculated risk—with your life, which you can resent if you want to—and risk the chance of your having to have surgery twice more, in order to avoid the certainty of having it once more, because I know you're in a hurry to get going again. Right now, if I were to have my guess, I'd say you feel very close to crying. Would I be right?"

"Is it that obvious?"

"I'm not even looking at you, which you'd know, if you were looking at me. No, you woke up feeling euphoric and damn Jack Boyd had to throw a clod in the churn. So now you'll be feeling as down as you did up. Don't worry about it. You'll be having some pretty drastic mood swings for a while. It's just part of recovering. Cry if you want to. It won't hurt you."

"I don't want to, now." And that is a damned lie, he thought. But he asked, forcing his voice to stay steady, "What can I expect, then? I should already have asked."

"Or I should have told you, but I figured to wait until you asked. Okay. By Thursday evening, barring any setbacks, you can start eating some really smooth, light solids. It won't be much, just stuff like puddings and light fruit. And I'm going to have to watch you real close to see how you handle it because if you're going to have trouble, that's one of the times it's likely to start."

"Then what?"

"If you go on handling everything without any trouble, you may be able to go home by next Wednesday if somebody else will drive you home and kind of look after you, and if you'll really go on taking it easy and resting enough. But you can start now getting mild exercise, like walking a little farther every day, just as long as you don't let yourself get too hot or tired. If everything goes all right, you'll be feeling about back to normal in around two and a half to three months. That's partly a matter of your luck and partly a matter of how well you do as you're told and don't try to get ahead of schedule. By the way, aren't you getting a little tired of having a wet bandage?"

"I'm getting damn tired of having a wet bandage. I was going to mention it, actually."

***

• *127* •

Nobody came to visit him all day. He was sick of reading. By one o'clock he was reduced to trying to watch soap operas; he turned the television back off at one-fifteen, back on at one-twenty, and off again at one-thirty. At two he sent a Grey Lady for a stack of comic books; at three, having read every Superman and Batman in the hospital, he started reading the Gideon Bible, which put him to sleep when he reached the "begats." He woke up at three-thirty, took a walk, and returned to bed tired, headachy, and sore by four.

When Cheryl came in at five it took some self-control for him not to snap at her. "What's the matter?" she asked.

He told her what was the matter.

"I'm sorry, Allen," she said.

"I'm sorry I'm so crabby," he answered. "What's happening in the real world?"

"Dovie Ledbetter's dead. They found her hanging in her cell last night about nine-thirty. Rick said she was looking out the cell window at some man about seven-fifteen, but he wasn't paying any attention and didn't really notice who."

"Damn!" Allen said violently. "Damn this bastard to hell anyway! And I suppose there's no word at all on Darling Corey?"

"You suppose right." She covered her face. "I am so tired," she said. "They called me out on Dovie because of it being partly my case and because the uniform men weren't altogether sure it was just suicide."

"Was it?"

"Yes. She managed to hang herself with her bra, tied through the window bars. Heaven only knows how; you'd think the cloth would have ripped from her weight, but it didn't."

"How late were you out?"

"I got to bed about two. And back up at six."

"Then what are you doing here?"

"I'm too tired to drive home. And I'm darn sure too tired to drive to Mama's to get Holly and then drive home."

"I would say crawl up here beside me, but I'm afraid that would shock the nurses."

"There's not room anyway."

"I'd make room."

"It's a temptation. But sure as anything I'd land my elbow just where you don't need anything landed right now."

"That is a consideration," Allen admitted. "I withdraw the invitation. Cheryl, go home and get some rest. I'm okay."

"How many visitors have you had today?"

"That doesn't matter," he said.

"You've been living in this area just a month. You hardly know anybody yet. So you figure I should just leave you all by yourself all the time?"

"Then tell me some more of what's happening in the real world."

"Nothing," she said. "Allen, it's just completely nothing. The lab people have gone back to Tennessee; Rick's the only one of them left, and he's packing up. The FBI went home yesterday. McCain's crew has followed up on every single check. All the ID's are phony. Two stores have that kind of camera that takes a simultaneous picture of the check, the ID, and the person. Those two stores cashed one check each. One of them is Dovie, and the other has her left hand over her face and her right thumb on the driver's license picture. Rick looked at the photos of the ID and said it looked like a combination of cut-and-paste, offset press, and a photo ID machine, probably Polaroid. McCain called the Polaroid people, and they said there are seventeen Polaroid ID machines in the area and they'd mail us particulars. Red and that guy that rides with him—"

"Keith?" Allen interrupted.

"Yeah, Keith. Red and Keith checked every print shop around and can't find anything that looks funny. The store people don't remember anything. Well, why should they? They cash fifty dozen checks a day; why should they remember one certain check two months later? McCain won't discuss what you were watching at Caddo Springs, but he says it hasn't been touched. Allen, if it wasn't for Dovie hanging herself, I'd say he's gone."

"Is Rick sure she was looking at somebody?"

"He says yes. He says she acted scared and stepped back real fast."

"And he didn't look to see who she was scared of? That's unlike Rick."

"He did look. And he says there were about twelve men there, and they were all acting normal."

"Has he been hypnotized?"

"Yes. He still says there were about twelve men there, and they were all acting normal. All he added was that some of them were black and some of them were white and half of them were wearing blue jeans and two of them were chewing tobacco." Absentmindedly, this time not in the least interested in Allen's reaction, Cheryl began to unbraid her hair as she talked. "So we tried to figure out who they were. There were four reporters, two black and two white. A deputy sheriff—black, out of uniform—was bringing Terry back from being arraigned."

"That same night?"

"The judge was going fishing. And Terry wanted out on bond." She was now rebraiding her hair. "We've got one wino placed there; he's white. That leaves three black men and two white men we can't place."

"And that's no use," Allen said.

"Of course it's no use. There's a bar half a block over, and it starts filling up about dark. The others were probably headed there. The wino had just gotten kicked out."

"Cheryl," Allen said, "go home and get some rest. Let me try to do some thinking. I haven't really been able to think much today. I've been too depressed."

"About not being able to eat?"

"About everything." Suddenly the violent urge to cry was back. "Just about everything. I guess I'm not really depressed. I guess I'm mad." He thought about it. "All right, I *am* mad. I'm furious. And I want to know who I'm furious at."

"I think it's pretty reasonable for you to feel that way," Cheryl answered. "We'll find out who it is. McCain's not going to learn any more. He's at a dead end, just following up things to say he's doing something. Sooner or later he'll have to give up and go home and by that time you'll be up and around again. Give all this ruckus time to die down, and we'll go out and clear the case."

"Sounds fine to me," Allen said. "Cheryl, I'm glad you came, but go home and get some rest now. Please? I don't want you to be as tired as you look right now."

"Okay," Cheryl said. She hugged him very briefly and left.

Allen lay awake a while after she left, thinking about anger. Finally he went to sleep, not very content with broth and Jello for supper but trying to cooperate.

Darling Corey wasn't asleep and she wasn't dancing. Out of sheer boredom, she had decided to watch the news. The face of the usual local newscaster was on the screen.

"The unusual concentration of federal officers in the little northeast Texas community of Lakeport is beginning to let up as two more postal inspectors returned today to their regional headquarters in Fort Worth. Inspector James McCain, in charge of the team investigating the weekend shooting of Inspector Allen Conyers, talked with Channel Six reporters tonight."

The television flickered, and the waiting face of the newsman was replaced by a rather tall, rather good-looking man with a ginger moustache and dark red hair. The voice of the unseen reporter asked, "Inspector McCain, does this withdrawal of a portion of your team indicate that the investigation is being terminated?"

"Definitely not," the man said. "This investigation will not be closed as long as the person who took the life of one federal law enforcement officer and seriously injured another is at large. I will repeat that a $10,000 reward is being offered for information leading to that person's arrest and conviction, and the driver of the vehicle used in the second shooting will be granted amnesty in return for testifying."

"Inspector McCain, are you saying that person will not even be arrested?"

"If that person will get in touch with me, or any law enforcement officer, he or she will be taken to a safe place where the suspect will not be able to follow. Assuming the suspect is then convicted, the person would receive the reward."

Darling Corey didn't hear the rest of the news. She was thinking of all the things she could buy for $10,000. First, of course, she'd get out of Caddo County. Dallas, that's where she would go, or maybe New York, or Hollywood. And she'd be a high-class call girl; she wouldn't have to put up with those drunk truck drivers and traveling salesmen any longer.

But first she'd have to figure out how to get the money, because one thing the Man didn't have was a telephone, or at least not one she could get at. He had one, but if he was leaving he unplugged it from the wall and put it in his closet, which locked with a key. Darling Corey couldn't get it open. She'd tried already, not to get at the phone, but just because she wanted to know what else he had in there.

And he'd taken to locking her in. She could maybe climb out a window, but he lived way out in the country, and she didn't know how she'd get anywhere because he'd taken her car keys.

Sure as anything, if he saw her walking he'd kill her. And she couldn't do nothing about it because he'd taken her gun. She didn't like not having no gun. People without guns get hurt.

That was a problem to think about.

And she had plenty of time to think because she'd been locked in all day. He'd said he had things to do. Well, that was true, he did. But he didn't have to lock her in! She wasn't going no place!

Conveniently forgetting going some place was exactly what she wanted to do, she lit another cigarette with the white sparkle in it and lay down to consider the matter. Only she went to sleep again.

Cheryl was right. Jim McCain had run out of leads and that fact didn't help his temper much. Cheryl, still working with him, caught a lot of the flak, although she suspected his unfortunate work team caught a lot more. Rick Harvey left to fly back to California. Lakeport was nearly back to normal, with only two postal inspectors besides McCain left of the horde of federal agents that had poured in. John Arnold, back in his store on Monday morning, answered McCain's insistent questioning by saying, "I didn't go to Shreveport this time. I went to Dallas. Is there any law says a man can't change his mind about where he wants to go get drunk?"

"No," McCain said, "but—"

"Look, McCain, if I wanted somebody keeping up with my whereabouts I'd get married again, but you aren't in the running. You're the wrong sex and color and you're too damn arrogant. And I never thought I'd say this to any cop at all whatsoever under any circumstances, but to you I'm saying it. Get out of my store. I don't like you. If you come back, come back with some sort of warrant that gives you the right to be here because this store is private property, and I see an officer right near you and I might have to ask her to arrest you for trespassing, much as I'd hate to inconvenience the lady by saddling her with a prisoner like you. Go. Now! Get the hell out of my store!"

McCain didn't like it. But he went.

Allen, hearing about it from Cheryl, laughed. "I'm glad to hear it," he said. "It was high time somebody gave McCain a little of what he dishes out, though I'll have to say I never saw him acting like this before. Do you know John's phone number?"

"No, but I'll look it up for you."

The gist of the ensuing conversation seemed to be that John could not visit Allen in the hospital that night because he already had plans made, but he'd be up there the next day.

"That's good," Cheryl said, "because I have to be in court all day, and I'd hate for you to have no company at all."

"What do you have to be in court on?"

"A stupid car theft that I was unfortunate enough to clear. Jerry Dakle and Sonny Davis were arguing because Jerry was dancing with Sonny's wife at a honky-tonk, and Jerry got too mad to stay there any longer. So he took Jerry's car keys, and left in Jerry's car, and promptly wrecked it. And unlucky me, I was on evening watch at the time and got to be the one to drag Sonny out of the car."

"How drunk was he?"

"I don't know; he passed out before we got him to the Intoximeter."

Allen laughed. "When I think of what I missed by not being a city cop, I don't even feel too bad about being shot. How long will your case take in court?"

"I told you, all day."

"What's the chance of it going into Wednesday?"

"I don't expect it to, but I guess it could. Why?"

"Because I'll probably get out of the hospital about noon Wednesday, and I figured on asking you to take me home. And will you go by my house and get me some clothes? I've got the nerve to do a lot of things, but I draw the line at being driven down a public street in a bathrobe. Cheryl, do you know I haven't worn a single thing but that bathrobe and my birthday suit in over a week?"

"I did sort of wonder," Cheryl said. "I guess it's lucky I got you the bathrobe, then, huh?"

"Really. Because if you hadn't I'd have had to give in and wear that damn hospital gown thing, and it's white with purple bands at the bottom. Why purple, I asked, and nobody would tell me."

"Probably couldn't. Hospitals are like that. But seriously, though, are you sure you're going to be able to manage anything around your waist?"

"Jack says yes."

"Jack?"

"Boyd. Doctor. He calls me Allen, I call him Jack. Fair exchange, I say."

"I never yet have managed to call a doctor by his first name," Cheryl confessed. "I think it's some kind of taboo."

"They're people, just like the rest of us. I think he likes it."

"Probably does," Cheryl said. "Allen, I have to go pick up Holly."

"Can you come back?"

"Uh-uh. I've got some things to do. I'll get back tomorrow afternoon if I get out of court in time, but I don't really expect to. I'll call though, anyhow."

"Okay," Allen said. "Kiss me good-bye?" He said it lightly so that she could treat it as a joke if she wanted to because she'd only kissed him once and that time he was fairly sure it was out of pity.

But to his surprise she leaned over, touched his lips with hers, and didn't back away immediately.

She went on home then, leaving him with another frustration to add to the others. But after a while he reflected, oh, well, right now, if she would, I couldn't. Not right now.

Trying to feel philosophical, he turned on the television.

"I got an idea," Darling Corey said.

"What kind of idea you got?" the Man asked lazily.

Twisting the silver bracelet around her wrist, Darling Corey proposed, "Let's go to a motel tonight." She'd been thinking about it for days, how to get to a phone, and finally she'd thought, motels have phones. And he couldn't watch her all the time. Oh, he could, but he wouldn't.

"What do you want to go to a motel for?" the Man asked. "Don't you have everything right here?"

She thought, wildly, what don't I have? "Swimming!" she improvised. "If we went to a motel, I could go swimming."

"You don't even have a bathing suit."

"You could get me one," she urged. "A bikini! A red one! How'd I look in a red bikini? Or maybe a black one?"

"Or maybe one of each?" he teased. He was watching her. "I'll tell you what. Tomorrow I'll get you a bathing suit. A bikini if I can find one. A red one, or a black one, or maybe one of each. And then we'll decide about going to a motel."

"Oh, baby, take me with you to get it!"

"Now, you know I can't do that. Them inspectors, they're looking for you, and the cops are, and everybody. Because they know you were with Jimmie when that shoot-out started. If they find you, you'll be in jail."

"Then how am I gonna get to a motel?" she wailed.

"I'll take care of that," he promised. He could take care of it quite easily. The arrangements were already made; he'd made them as soon as he realized what McCain was trying to do. Post office people, he thought, they think they're so smart—

He remembered that part-time job his dad got him at the post office when he was in high school. That was the Christmas a lot of the carriers were out with the flu. It wasn't his fault that package had broken open. And anybody would have pocketed that gold chain once they'd seen it. But they fired him all the same and called his dad to come get him and his dad had beat him half senseless. Well, that was nothing new; his dad always slammed him around. But not in public like he did that time, right there in the back of the post office with the postmaster standing there watching.

Well, he was getting even. The post office was looking sillier than he had looked then, getting belted for stealing at sixteen. He'd stolen plenty from them, and there was plenty more to come. And he didn't mean to kill that first man; he'd shot because he was startled and because the man had been going for his gun. But it had been fun, when he thought about it, to kill somebody from the post office. So it had been fun, as well as practical, to go after Allen Conyers. And maybe he'd just have another try at him.

Pull another holdup now, he told himself, but not to shoot anybody this time. Keep them guessing. Keep them guessing, like his dad had always kept *him* guessing—whether he'd get beaten this time or whether his dad would think this shenanigan was funny.

They wanted Darling Corey, those cops? They'd get her. But not like they wanted her.

"Thanks for coming," Allen said. "I've really been wanting to talk with you."

"You I'll talk with," John answered, in that deep voice he had. "But if that son-of-a-bitch McCain comes around again, I may flatten his face for him."

"He does have pretty abrasive manners," Allen agreed.

"Abrasive is a mild word. Do you mind if I smoke?"

"I don't, but Cheryl does, and the smoke smell kind of stays around, you know."

"Okay." John put the package back in his pocket. "Look, does that fool think I'm involved in this sack of shit?"

"Yes, he does," Allen said. "But don't feel individually picked on. For a while he thought I was. And I'm not sure he's got me completely cleared in his mind yet."

"What the hell kind of an idiot is he? Does he think you shot yourself?"

"No, I think he thinks you shot me."

"Thinks I did? What for?"

"On account of a thieves' quarrel or something like that. He seems to think we were working together on it, to start with, and then I wanted out, or else you did, or some such matter. Or did think that; he might have changed his mind again and decided I wasn't in it and you shot me because you thought I might catch up to you."

"Oh," John said. "I'll have to digest that one a while. Why did you want to see me—to ask me if I shot you? Because if you did, I didn't."

"Cheryl assures me that if you had you'd have used a .45 and I wouldn't be in any position to be wondering who shot me."

"Cheryl's not necessarily right. What were you shot with?"

"A .32 Omega."

"Oh, shit." John reached in his pocket again. "Tell Cheryl if my smoke makes her hair smell, she can wash her hair when she gets home. Allen, I may be in trouble."

"Tell me about it."

"I bought a .32 Omega about eight years ago, before Carrie died. Carrie was my wife, and she was too little to use a .45. And as to why an Omega—it was no sort of gun at all, of course, but Carrie thought it was pretty." Both men grinned at that. "After she died I kept it in the car. About two years ago somebody stole it. I figured, damn fool me, to leave the car unlocked, but what the hell, a .32 Omega. And I didn't bother to report it."

"You should have."

"I should have. Because if it turns out the ATF traces the gun you were shot with back to me—like I said, I may be in trouble." He blew smoke. "Those people that keep hollering about registering firearms, pro or con, don't seem to know they're already registered."

"People don't seem to know a lot of things," Allen agreed. "No, John, I don't think you shot me, and if it turns up your gun I still won't think so. What I wanted to talk to you about—look, from what Cheryl tells me, you've got a lot of influence. Isn't there any way you could talk one of those whores into telling you something?"

"You think I haven't been trying? I'll tell you what I wouldn't tell McCain. I should have told him, and I meant to, only he just makes me so damn mad. I wasn't drunk in Dallas last week; I haven't left Caddo County. I let my daughter think I was gone so she wouldn't get to wondering and worrying, but I've been in honky-tonks and bars and jukes all night and sleeping in the daytime in rinky-dink hotels ever since I turned on the radio Saturday morning and heard what happened to you. I've been hunting answers. And I'd even have told McCain if I'd gotten any answers. Only I didn't. I didn't get one damn thing."

"I appreciate your trying."

"And *I'm* scared, now," John said bitterly. "There's no reason why I should be. I haven't done a thing wrong, and I'm a retired colonel with a good military record. But I'm still black, and this is still the South, and it wouldn't be too hard for somebody to prove I lied about where I've been for nearly a week and a half. If it should turn out now that it was my gun—"

"Then I'll suddenly remember that I saw the person and it wasn't you," Allen said.

"McCain would know you were lying."

"Sure he would. But the jury wouldn't."

"Thanks for that," John said. "But let's hope it never comes to that. If anybody ever steals a gun from me again, you can bet I'll report it. Look, about—"

An hour later, John said, "I've got to go now. My daughter said she'd had all the store she could handle for a while."

After he left, Allen sat and brooded. He did trust John Arnold; he did; only—McCain said John was in Shreveport when Matt Elton was killed.

There were too many coincidences. And Allen Conyers didn't like coincidences.

Cheryl didn't come to see him that night. She called at eight-thirty to tell him she was sorry, she'd just gotten out of court, but at least the case had gone to the jury and she was *through* with it. And Sergeant Hall said she could come get him in a detective car tomorrow because it was bigger than her car and he'd have more room to stretch out. And she'd already gone to get him some groceries so they wouldn't have to stop anywhere; he could just go right home and wouldn't have time to get tired.

Allen told her he'd walked for a full hour that day in the morning and another full hour in the afternoon, plus other short walks, and he didn't think riding three miles or so in a good car sounded that tiring.

Cheryl said she'd see him about eleven tomorrow.

Allen wasn't tired enough to go to sleep. He went out in the hall to walk some more. His body told him that what he really wanted was Cheryl, but he told his body to shut up, he couldn't have Cheryl yet.

It's unreal, he thought, that even the sound of her voice—!

The Man had stolen the motel room key a week before. He'd learned quite by accident that this room had a plumbing problem; they never rented it unless every other room was full. From the number of cars, it was apparent that the place was only half full. That was what he had expected on a Tuesday night.

This room would do for Darling Corey. He'd let her have her swim.

·Nine·

Wearing clothes again didn't hurt, not even where the belt buckle pressed against the brand-new scar. And it was very pleasant to be sitting up again, in a moving car, outside in the sunshine. Cheryl glanced over at him and smiled. He smiled back. And the radio said, "Car 17, what's your ten-twenty?"

"Car 17 is ten-six," Cheryl said into the microphone.

"Car 17, Car 1 requests you immediately abandon present assignment and proceed directly to the County Line Motel."

She looked at Allen. "Go," he said. "I won't break. And I don't want you in trouble with your chief."

"Car 17 en route to the County Line Motel," she said resignedly. "But I don't have to speed going over there," she told Allen.

Sergeant Hall was standing in the parking lot. "Allen, I'm sorry as hell," he said, "and I'll get a patrol car to get you on home. But I needed Cheryl over here. We're trying to keep everything connected with this case assigned to the same people."

"What is it now?" Cheryl asked.

"It's Darling Corey," Hall said.

Allen opened his car door. "Cheryl can take me home later," he said.

"Allen, I know Dr. Boyd told you—"

"To take it easy. And I will. But this I want to look at. Hey, remember, I've never even seen her."

Darling Corey had put up a fight. The lemon-yellow fingernails were broken. But she'd been a small woman, even smaller than Cheryl, and the fight hadn't been good enough. She was on the floor, between the two beds in the room, wearing a bright red bikini. There were defense wounds on the outsides of her hands, and the hilt of the knife that had made them was protruding between her breasts. Cheryl pushed experimentally on her wrist.

"Yeah," Hall said softly. "I make it about eleven last night, give or take a few hours. You agree?"

"Uh-huh," Cheryl said. "And that makes it too late to try for latents on her skin even if we did have the stuff to do it with. I got Rick to tell me how in case we ever got a chance."

Allen felt reasonably sure that Cheryl had almost forgotten his presence. She was all cop now, squatting on the floor looking intently at the hilt of the knife, carefully not touching anything. "Well, I hope McCain is proud of himself," she said angrily. "I tried to tell him this would happen. All right, laugh if you want to, but I *am* sorry. Whatever else she was or wasn't, she was alive. People knew she was there."

"Yes, she was alive," Hall agreed somberly. "There'll be people cry at her funeral. But I always figured she'd end up like this."

"So did I," Cheryl said, "but not for this reason." She was fairly sure what the reason was; the telephone, installed before the days of phone jacks, had been ripped out of the wall. "Has McCain been notified?"

"He's on the way. Not that it's got a damn thing to do with him, except that obviously it's part of the same case. And Lloyd's en route to take pictures."

Cheryl went on looking at Darling Corey. Something was missing, and she couldn't figure out what. Examining the body more closely she noticed an abrasion on the left wrist. And that was it. Her bracelet. The wide silver bracelet she'd worn daily for years, the bracelet that had told them it had been Darling Corey driving the car the night Allen was shot, was gone.

Jim McCain walked in. "What the hell happened?"

"Your lure worked," Allen said. "She was stabbed trying to get to a telephone. Only problem is, you didn't catch anybody with it."

"You don't know that yet," McCain said. "Who registered for this room last night?"

"We haven't checked yet," Hall answered wearily. "Around Caddo County, we've got this limitation. We haven't figured out yet how to do more than one thing at a time."

"Well, I can find that out," McCain said and strode out. In a few minutes he was back. "Nobody signed for it last night, but there's a key missing. So I checked on who'd been in it the last couple of weeks.

It was mostly those damn reporters. But John Arnold had it three nights running. He wasn't drunk in Shreveport or Dallas. He was right here in Caddo County. If you won't get him in for questioning, I damn well will."

"He didn't do this, Jim," Allen answered. "And as to where he was, I already knew it. He told me yesterday."

McCain's head turned sharply. "When? When did he tell you?"

"Yesterday, I said, when he came up to my room."

"Why did he do that?"

"Because I called and asked him to."

"And he did."

"Yes, he did."

"And he told you he'd stayed in Caddo County last week. Did he tell you why?"

"Yes, he told me why. Would you like to know?"

Ignoring the question, McCain demanded, "Did he also tell you he owned a .32 Omega? Because the ATF told me this morning. I'd asked them to try to track down every one in Caddo County. That's the only one they could come up with that has been sold to anybody living in Caddo County in the last ten years. But he didn't tell you that, did he?"

"He told me he'd owned a .32 Omega, yes," Allen said wearily.

"Then what else did he tell you?" McCain demanded. "What else that you've kept to yourself?"

"He told me he was sick and tired of you and wished you'd get your ass back to Fort Worth!" Allen shouted. "And so do I! And he told me he'd like to flatten your face for you, and I feel the same way." With no warning whatever, his fist lashed out, catching McCain in the mouth. McCain staggered back a couple of steps, trying to keep his balance, and Hall quickly stepped in front of him, grabbing his upper arms.

Allen dropped to the floor, sitting on one knee panting, and glanced up. Cheryl knelt beside him. "Are you all right?" she asked.

"I'm fine," he answered, trying to get his breathing under control but quite unable to keep himself from grinning.

"You can let go of me just any time now," McCain said quietly.

"Okay," Hall said and let go. "I just figured you might need a little assistance for a minute in deciding whether to act on your judgment or your temper."

"I think I deserved that one," he answered, still quietly. He sat down on the floor beside Allen. "Having got that out of your system, would you also like to tell me my handling of the case has been highly unprofessional?"

"Do I need to tell you that?" Allen asked.

McCain wiped his mouth with the back of his hand. Then he got a handkerchief out of his pocket and wiped his mouth and the back of his hand. "I don't want to bleed on the crime scene," he said. "No, you don't need to tell me that. I'm well aware of it. But may I tell you why?"

"The main thing I know is that Cheryl has been catching a lot of the brunt of it," Allen said. "She's been trying not to complain, but enough is enough. I don't particularly care what your reason is."

McCain shrugged and got up. Allen looked at the set of his face and said, "Jim, I shouldn't have said that. Sit down. Tell me what's wrong. I know you couldn't have reached the position you hold today by acting the way you're acting now."

"You could also add I'm not going to keep holding the position I hold today if I keep acting the way I've been acting," McCain answered. "I know that, too. I should have asked to be removed from the case. I should never have tried to work it to start with. Because Matt Elton was a friend of my sister, a good friend. Oh, hell, I might as well tell the rest of the truth. He and my sister were engaged. When he got out of college he knew he wanted to go into federal law enforcement. He was talking about the FBI or the Secret Service. I talked him into coming with us."

"He could have been killed in either one of them."

"He could have been. But he wasn't."

"So you felt guilty, and you took your guilt out by trying to make me look guilty. And you felt like you couldn't trust yourself because you let your sister's fiancé get killed, so you couldn't trust me. And you were too emotionally involved to think straight, so you jumped on Cheryl for being emotionally involved."

"That's about the size of it."

"I won't say I'm sorry I punched you," Allen stated, "because I'm not sorry and I won't lie and say I am. But I'll say I apologize. And I'll admit that wasn't real professional behavior either."

"I won't say I'll go back to Fort Worth and leave it with you," McCain answered, "because I can't, not now, when I've gone this far on it. But I would if I could. And I can say I'll try to be a little more human." He held out his hand. "The apology is accepted," he added, "and I don't expect you to be sorry. Officially, we'll forget it happened."

"Thanks," Allen said, and shook his hand briefly. "Okay, about John. I called him up to the hospital to see if I could get some answers, since I knew you had him thoroughly riled. Jim, he's been in intelligence most of his adult life. He's like us. He's on our side. Treat him as a suspect, and he's just like me. He'll take it just so long, and then he's angry. Treat him as a pro, and he'll work with you all the way. He didn't go home at all last week because he wanted his daughter to think he was out of town so she wouldn't worry about him. He was bar crawling, hunting information. He stayed at this motel and one other. And he didn't get the information he went after, and he feels bad about it."

"And the gun?"

"He says it was stolen and he neglected to report it."

"And you really, honest to God, believe him?"

"I believe him, Jim. Look, I know I'm not as good an investigator as you, under most circumstances, are. But I do understand people reasonably well. And I know I'm not as driven as you are to find out who got Elton because I hardly knew Elton. But I feel very damned personal about finding out who put a bullet into my gut because I'm the only me I've got. If I could see any reason at all to suspect John Arnold, I'd go right on suspecting him until either he was cleared or it was proven to be somebody else. Well, I don't know who shot me. I wish I did know. But this I do know: it was not John Arnold."

"All right," McCain said. "I guess I have to accept that. Allen, let me take you home. These people have a murder to work. And we weren't trained in working murders, and you need some rest."

"That sounds like a reasonable suggestion," Allen said. "Cheryl? Call me when you get time."

"I'll be there," she said vaguely, her mind clearly far from him.

In the car, Allen thought about what it would really be like to be married to Cheryl. He'd never wondered, before meeting Cheryl, how it would feel to know somebody might decide to shoot at someone he loved. And he'd never thought about how it would feel to need somebody who couldn't be there because she had to do something else. Not that Lisa had always been there, but she was usually gone because she wanted to be gone, not because she had to be, and he'd assumed without ever thinking about it at all that if he really, really needed her she'd be there.

But now he needed Cheryl and she couldn't come because she had a case to work—partly his case, which was even worse.

He wondered what it was he thought he had that Cheryl needed from him. She didn't need him to support her; she could support herself. She didn't need him to defend her; she could defend herself. Probably she didn't need his love at all because she'd gotten by perfectly happily without his love, or anybody else's, for years. Probably she didn't need *him* at all; probably it was all arrogance on his part to think he could make her need him the way he needed her.

On the other hand, of course, he didn't need her for most of the traditional reasons either. He'd lived alone for five years and he hadn't starved. His clothes were in perfectly good shape, and if his place wasn't spotless, well, neither was Cheryl's. No, the reasons he needed her were a lot more involved.

He leaned his head against the car window. He didn't want to go home, because that apartment wasn't really home at all; he didn't have a home. He knew what it would be like—hot and untidy and smelling of stale air and his old cigarette smoke; just an empty, loveless place to sleep. He hoped he didn't look as desolate as he felt.

"Allen? Do you want me to come in with you?"

"No, you have work to do. Thanks for the lift." And damn, he'd left the new bathrobe and the two plants in the back seat of Cheryl's car. Well, she'd probably bring them by later.

Bracing himself for the sight of the untidiness he'd left behind almost two weeks earlier, he unlocked the door.

The air conditioner was humming softly, and the room was cool. The smell of lemon-scented furniture and something cooking had replaced the stale cigarette smoke. He followed the second smell to a crock pot that must be Cheryl's, with soup steaming in it. The only thing on the coffee table, where he'd left plates and glasses and old newspapers, was a crayon drawing of flowers, signed in very large straggling blue letters, "Love from Holly." He dropped his shirt, already damp with the sweat of exhaustion, into a completely empty clothes hamper, and he knew before he turned back the covers that he'd find clean sheets there. With everything else she's had to do, he thought. With everything else that's been on her mind. And he went to sleep feeling as comforted as if she'd been there.

***

Jim McCain parked his car and sat in it for a moment. This wasn't the easiest thing he'd ever done in his whole entire life, and maybe it wasn't totally necessary, but right now he saw it as necessary. Reminding himself that if he wouldn't keep losing his temper he would not have to apologize so often, he got out of the car and went to the door. "Colonel Arnold," he said, "may I come in?"

Arnold looked at him. "I'm out of the Army," he said. "Yeah, come on in."

"I just wanted to come and apologize," McCain said. "I've been inexcusably rude to you. I haven't treated you as a fellow professional, and I haven't behaved in a professional manner myself. I have no right whatsoever to ask you for any kind of help, but for Allen Conyers's sake, and for the sake of a dead man I cared a lot about, I'm asking you anyway."

"When you put it that way," John Arnold said promptly, "I'll do what I can. What do you need?"

"You told Allen your .32 Omega was stolen. When did that happen?"

"It'll be two years ago this fall. I don't remember exactly when; I'd guess October or November."

"Why didn't you report it then? It would sure have helped a lot now if you had."

"I realize that, and of course I should have. But I felt so damn stupid leaving a gun in the unlocked glove box of an unlocked car."

"We all get careless at times," McCain said, and then was afraid that might sound patronizing. He went on hastily, "Had you made a habit of keeping it in the car?"

"Oh, yes, I'd had it there for years."

"Who all would have known it?"

John made an expansive gesture. "Everybody, just about," he said. "I don't make any secret of my habits. I try to make sure everybody does know I keep guns around; I figure that'll make it less likely I'll ever have to use them."

"Had you ever fired it?"

John raised his eyebrows. "What good is a gun you don't shoot? Of course I'd fired it."

"Where?"

"What do you mean?"

• 145 •

"I mean, do you use a public range or go out and shoot behind a hill, or what? And is it a place lots of people use, or mostly just you?"

"You going for a test slug?"

"Yes. If we could say it *is* your gun, then we'd have a terminus of sorts. We'd be able to say he almost certainly was in Caddo County in the fall two years ago, just before all this broke out."

"Unless somebody else stole it and he then acquired it from that person."

"That's why I said 'almost,' " McCain said.

"Okay. I shoot out on the creek. I doubt anyone else has been using a .32 out there; I've seen a lot of .22's and .38's and a few .45's besides mine, but no .32's." He gave careful directions and added, "If you can't find the place, come back and I'll close up for a couple of hours and take you out there."

"Thanks," McCain said and turned to go.

"Hey, McCain!"

He turned. "Yeah?"

"Here, take this with you. It's hot out there." Arnold tossed him a can of Coke and added, grinning, "You look like you've been plenty hot already."

"Yeah," McCain said wryly. "Thanks. I'll let you know what kind of results we get."

"You do that."

"There should be more to do," Cheryl said.

"Well, there's not, right now," Hall answered. "But I know what you mean. We didn't really care that much about Dovie because we didn't really know Dovie. But no matter how much of a pest Darling Corey was, she had a place in our lives. We knew her; we knew what to expect of her; and now she's gone, and as stupid as it sounds to say it, after all she's done, we'll be missing her for a while."

Jim McCain came in, rather dirty and somewhat sweaty, in his usual hurry. "Ken," he said, "is there somebody you could spare to go to Garland?"

"Why do you want somebody to go to Garland?"

"John Arnold and I have been out digging where he does his practice firing. We've got some old slugs from his .32. If the lab can say the slug that hit Allen came from the gun stolen from Arnold, then we've got another angle to look at. If not, then there's one angle we *don't* have to follow up." Hall stared at him and he added defensively, "Well, you said your lab man is good; I'm taking your word for it."

The silence continued, and he burst out, "Look, damn it, don't you see? We don't know, right now, whether we're looking for somebody from Texas, or Arkansas, or Louisiana, or none of the above. But if he took a gun out of John Arnold's car nearly two years ago, the chances are he lives in or around Lakeport. And if he lives in or around Lakeport and has some reason to know the other two areas as well as he clearly does, well, that could give us something else to go on. It could put us way ahead."

"Package up your evidence," Hall said. "I'll get somebody to take it up tomorrow."

"What's everybody staring at me for?" McCain demanded.

"Go look in the mirror," Cheryl advised.

His mouth was swollen and his lower lip was cut; blood had caked on it. Dirt was clinging in beads to the sweat in the creases of his neck and to his upper lip. He returned to the detective bureau washed, but his eyes defied anybody to mention the state of his mouth. Only nobody did, and finally he said, "All right, I know what I look like. I said I had it coming and I did. Now just forget it."

Hall got up and slapped him on the shoulder. "You're human after all," he said. "It's after hours. Come on, I'll buy you a beer."

"In a minute," McCain said. "You know what we haven't followed up?"

"What?" Cheryl asked.

"Those photo ID machines. Polaroid gave us a list of the ones in the area. Tomorrow, let's divide up and go look at all of them."

"What's that going to tell us?"

"I don't know if it'll tell us anything," McCain said. "But let's look, anyway."

The phone rang, and Hall reached for it. "Yeah?" he said.

"Somebody just stuck up the main post office," the dispatcher told him. Hall relayed the news.

"Oh my God!" McCain said. "Anybody hurt?"

"They didn't say. You coming with me?"

"I'll take my car," McCain said.

Nobody was hurt.

There was no use dusting for prints. The lone gunman had been wearing, in Texas in June with the mercury sitting at ninety-eight degrees, a green ski mask and leather gloves, a long-sleeved flannel shirt, khaki pants, and work boots. Nobody could tell if the person was male or female, black or white—only that an obviously disguised voice had demanded cash, stamps, and money orders, and that the robber had left with a filled paper bag. They'd heard a car start, but nobody could get to the door fast enough to see what kind of car.

"Estimate of losses? Are you kidding?" a postal clerk demanded. "It'll take at least two hours to figure that out."

There was virtually nothing for anybody to do there. And there was certainly nothing to look at. But already, there were two reporters taking pictures. Waymon, as usual, was using a telephoto lens to circumvent the uniform man at the door keeping people out.

"I have to have statements from everybody that was in the post office," McCain said, trying very hard to control his temper, since he obviously could do nothing about reporters outside. "There's a dictating machine in Allen's office. Cheryl, do you mind helping me by getting the statements while I interview people before they actually give statements?"

"Glad to help," Cheryl answered.

"Ken, would you see to it your people are notified of what we're looking for?"

"I'll get a supplemental lookout on the air."

But they all knew, without anybody saying it, that nowhere in Caddo County was there now a man wearing a green ski mask and leather gloves.

For now, the apartment felt like a real home. Holly was lying back on the floor, holding a plush bear over her head and talking to it. Allen was still eating with great care, but Cheryl had produced (apparently by magic, because it didn't seem she'd been in the kitchen a total of five minutes) baked chicken breasts and asparagus to go with the soup Allen found he'd already eaten half of.

"What do you call this soup?" he asked. "I like it."

"I call it lemon soup, because that's its name. But it's really more of a chicken soup. And I'm glad you like it. I like it too." Her voice sounded detached.

"Cheryl, is something wrong?"

"Not really," she said. "But—oh, I was just thinking about something you said to McCain. You told him he felt guilty and that he was taking it out on you. And I just got to thinking, maybe I'm like that. You know, what I told you about? I couldn't have prevented it, either time, but I felt guilty anyway, like it was somehow really my fault. But—I'd thought I just didn't like—you know—because of him, but maybe it's because of me feeling guilty.'' She glanced at Holly, who was sitting on the floor totally absorbed in a television show. "This would be a lot easier to explain somewhere else.''

"You don't need to explain it,'' Allen answered. "I understand what you're saying. But whether you feel angry or whether you feel guilty, it's in the past. Just let go of it. You can protect yourself now. Hell, you can protect *me*. If I'd gone alone to talk to Darling Corey I don't think I'd have gotten out alive. The past is over. Let it go.''

"Can you do that?'' she asked. "Can you let go of what Lisa did?''

"Now I can,'' he answered. "And I was doing the same thing as you, Cheryl, only it was anger I couldn't handle. I tried not to be angry at Lisa, so I was depressed. I tried not to be angry at McCain—I even tried not to be angry at whoever shot me. You got me through that. You let me know it was all right to be angry.''

"So you punched McCain.''

"So I punched McCain. Which was overreacting, but I'm still not really sorry I did it. I don't know—maybe what I'm trying to say is, don't you go on overreacting. I won't punch McCain again. And you shouldn't feel guilty about anything to do with me. You helped me more than you'll ever know. Can't I help you now?''

"I don't know how to let you,'' Cheryl answered. "But I'll think about it.''

"Are you still afraid of me, Cheryl?'' Allen asked gently.

"I don't *know*,'' Cheryl said wretchedly.

"Cheryl—you're a good cop. And you're a good mother to Holly. And the things you've done for me—make me feel—secure.'' His mouth curled briefly; that was an odd word to use to describe a clean house and a pot of soup. But he continued, "You do the things a woman does. But every time you start feeling the way a woman feels you freeze up. And then you want to go to the kitchen or turn back into a cop. Cheryl, I'm not wearing my gun and ID now. I'm a man. That's all. And you're not wearing your gun and ID now. You're a woman. Don't be afraid of being a woman.''

"It hurts to be a woman,'' she whispered.

"It hurts to be a man,'' he answered quietly. "For over five years, every time I saw a child the age mine would have been I felt like somebody was tearing my insides out of me. Does it frighten you when I look at Holly, when I hold Holly?''

''Yes. And I know that's not right, because I know you wouldn't—'' She stopped, looking beseechingly at him.

''Wouldn't do to her what someone did to you?'' His voice stayed completely steady. ''No. I wouldn't. I love her, Cheryl. All the love I saved for so long for a child who never was born is hers now. And the way that I love you now tells me I never really loved Lisa at all. That's love you can't accept yet. But it's there when you're ready for it. I'm not asking for your love yet. Just tell me when it's there for me.''

''It may never be.''

''I'll take that chance. I have no choice now, Cheryl. I can't decide not to love you.''

''And that hurts you.''

''Yes,'' Allen said, ''it does. It hurts to love and not be loved. But that's a hurt I accept, and I don't blame you for it. I'm a man, and I love you, and I'm not asking for anything from you that you don't want to give me.''

''Not even a kiss?''

''Not even a kiss,'' he told her soberly.

Cheryl looked at him, really looked at him, at the thinning brown hair, the quiet blue eyes, the tan that was fading because of the time in the hospital. He was not a tall man; he was taller than Cheryl, but Sergeant Hall, at six feet two, towered over him when they stood side by side. He wasn't fat, but he weighed a little more than he should and the extra weight wasn't muscle. He was a man who was entering middle age, and he looked it. He didn't look threatening; he didn't look frightening. There was an appeal in his eyes that she didn't know how to understand.

She'd kissed him before. But she didn't want to kiss him tonight because she was in his house and she had cooked his supper and washed his clothes, and a kiss might seal something she didn't want to seal. ''It's past Holly's bedtime,'' she said hastily. ''I'll just go wash the dishes and—''

Allen chuckled softly. ''There, you're doing it again,'' he said. ''Never mind. I can wash the dishes. You get Holly on home if it's past her bedtime. Good night, Cheryl. Thank you for supper. It was good.''

***

"Are you all right, Cheryl?" Sergeant Hall asked. "You don't look to me like you're getting enough rest."

"I just didn't get much sleep last night, that's all."

"Because Allen's home?" Lloyd suggested slyly.

"Don't be an idiot," Cheryl said. "He's got about fifty-seven stitches in his abdomen; I know because he told me. You think he's fool enough to want to come unsewed—even all other considerations aside?"

"I was just kidding," Lloyd protested.

"Well, don't kid me today. I feel rotten."

McCain and the two remaining members of his team came in; Mc-Cain had twelve sheets of paper in his hand.

"Are those what we talked about last night?" Hall asked.

"Yeah, how do you want us to team up on it?"

"I'll take Keith out of your office, Lloyd can go with Red, and Cheryl with you. Each of us can cover four locations. You want to explain or want me to?"

"You go ahead." McCain, clearly, was making a determined effort to be human.

"Okay. For those of you who don't know, we have been assured by the document examiner that the phony ID we've seen photos of was probably made on a Polaroid identification machine. Polaroid has supplied us with the names of the owners of all those in this area. Several of them we've tentatively ruled out for various reasons, but we are having a look at twelve of them. While you're there, look for anything that seems suspicious or even unusual. Also, find out who has access to the machines. All right?"

McCain handed out the sheets. "As the man said, these aren't all that Polaroid told us about. But these are the ones we're looking at now."

At two-thirty, a hot, tired group was back in the detective bureau. Into the gloom, Cheryl said, "I know where there's one that wasn't even on the list."

"Where?" McCain asked.

She took her identification card out of her pocket. "This was made on a Polaroid," she said.

"But we changed systems a couple of years ago," Hall said. "I don't even think that's still around."

"Sure it is."

"Where?" McCain asked.

"Where?" Hall echoed. "I sure didn't know it was still around."

"In a closet in the county commission meeting chamber," she said. "I guess that was the most out-of-the-way place they could think of to store it. Shall we go look at it?"

Hall shrugged. "The meeting room'll be locked."

"Maybe not," she said.

"And anyway, if it's open the closet will be locked."

"Maybe—not," McCain said, getting out of his chair with a chill feeling of foreboding. The report from Garland had been brought back half a hour earlier; they knew, now, that a reputable firearms examiner had identified the old slug from John Arnold's .32 as having been fired from the same gun that had wounded Allen Conyers and killed Matt Elton. They weren't hunting an anonymous .32 Omega now; they were hunting a known .32 Omega with a known serial number and a known background. "Maybe it won't be locked. Cheryl, let's you and me have a look."

The door to the commission chamber opened easily. So did the storage closet door. The ID machine was there, with a plastic dust cover over it, looking as if it had never been touched. But it took Jim McCain under two minutes to find, on a closet shelf in the court house, the paper bag containing counterfeit forms for Texas, Louisiana, and Arkansas driver's licenses.

Nobody entered the room for the next day and a half except county police, postal inspectors, Texas Rangers, and Rick Harvey, who was hurriedly flown back.

"What did you find?" McCain asked, when Rick, grimy with fingerprint powder and red-eyed from lack of sleep and too frequent changes of time zone, finally came out.

"What the hell did you expect me to find?" the usually eventempered document examiner replied. "I didn't find one damn thing. The bastard covers his tracks."

"They why did he leave the blanks there?" Lloyd demanded.

"Can you think of a better place?" Cheryl asked. "So we've found the blanks. So we know he has access to a print shop. We already knew he had access to a print shop. We haven't found the print shop, so he can get new blanks. We've found this ID machine, but he can always round up another. And if we knew who he was and searched his house and car tomorrow, we couldn't tie him to it because he hasn't got the blanks. Or, probably, anything else.''

"He's laughing at us," McCain said. "He didn't get five hundred dollars out of the post office, and he dumped everything but cash. He didn't expect much of a haul there, but he always robs post offices as his last act before leaving town, so he robbed that one. He wasn't out for what he could get, that time. He was just telling us good-bye. And now he's gone. And we don't know where he'll surface next time, or what he'll do next time, or—God help us—who he'll kill next time. But he's through here. And we missed him. And what's most infuriating is that he's not even a smart crook. He's thing smart, but he's people stupid. It'll be a people mistake that'll catch him. I'd hoped he'd make it here. But he didn't.''

Nobody answered.

Nobody disagreed.

"I'm going home," Cheryl said. She made two phone calls. One was to her mother, to arrange for Holly to stay the night, and one was to Allen, to say she wasn't coming over. "I'm off tomorrow," she said to Hall. "Don't let anybody call me out tonight.''

"Okay," he said. "I won't let anybody call me out tonight either.''

·*Ten*·

Jim McCain had been back in Fort Worth for a week. Crime in Caddo County had dropped to about the same as usual—burglary, theft, vandalism, and not much else. Allen Conyers had been to the doctor that morning, and the doctor had been encouraging. In fact, he'd said Allen could begin to work half a day and build up to a full day as fast as he felt like it.

Allen left the doctor's office and returned to his car. He hadn't been wearing his gun, but since he was now officially working he took it out of his glove box and threaded his belt through the holster. He felt better, emotionally, with that familiar weight on his right hip; he'd lived with it for so many years that not wearing it made him feel naked.

He drove to his office, where his part-time secretary (he was allowed ten hours of secretary a week) was sitting at her desk reading a paperback book. She seemed rather startled to see him. But as she had been hired only two days before he was shot, and had actually reported to work under McCain instead of under him, he didn't have much to say to her now. That little bit said, he went to opening mail.

Henry Warner's Social Security check (enclosed) had been stolen out of his mail box and cashed at Ward's by, according to the driver's license information written on the back of the check, a white male. Probably an isolated occurrence not related to the recent crime wave.

Janet Carson had a letter from somebody in Wyoming wanting to sell her tickets to the Canadian National Lottery; was it legal? Yes, in Canada, but not in the U.S. mail from Wyoming to Texas.

A couple of very ordinary scams and one rather interesting scam he'd better call the Fraud Division in Fort Worth about.

Allen Conyers was home, and he was happy to be home.

After a while, he got in his car and drove to the police station. Cheryl, in the detective bureau with her back to him, was saying patiently, "But *then* what happened? You're telling me the same thing over and over. I understand that you were upset, but I need you to tell me what happened after that."

Ken Hall, apparently a not too interested spectator, glanced up and saw Allen. He stood up, grinning. "You're back in harness? It's great to see you!"

"It's great to be back in harness," Allen answered.

"You need something or just visiting?"

"Need to borrow Cheryl when she's got time," Allen said. "We'd made up our minds that once McCain went home and I was able to work again, and everything was about back to normal, we were going to put our heads together and solve this case. I'm ready to start on it."

"Come on back to my office." Inside, Hall asked, "Allen, are you sure you want to borrow Cheryl? Could you really work with her now? I realize in most situations you could, but—if you were under fire again? You could treat her as another cop right after you met her, but could you now?"

"I had to think that one through," Allen said. "Yes, I could. I'd be terrified out of my mind to be under fire right now, after what I've been through this month. But I thought—well, does Cheryl have the right to choose her own life-style? Of course she does, and she chose her job with her eyes open. And then I thought, could Cheryl stand what I've been through? Of course she couldn't—but Ken, I couldn't stand it either, and I had to stand it all the same. So would she if she had to. So the only other question is, could I stand to see it? My emotional reaction is, no I couldn't. But I could if I had to."

"So you'd put women in combat."

"I wouldn't put anybody in combat if I could get out of it. But if I'm in combat I'd rather have somebody I trust beside me than somebody I don't. And she'd rather be there than not be there. You know that's true."

"And if she was killed?"

"I would rather die myself. That's my gut reaction, of course. But when you think that through, it's utter selfishness. It's saying, I'd rather be safe and leave her hurt, than to have her safe and me hurt."

"So you consider a dead person to be safe?"

"I think we've just had a communications breakdown."

"I think we have too," Hall said. "It sounded to me like you just said a dead person is safe. What do you mean, safe?"

"Are you one of those people who think when you die that's all?"
Allen asked, aghast.

"You mean you're one of those nuts who don't think that?"

"No," Allen said, "I don't. And do you ever have a surprise coming
when you wake up the morning after you die."

Hall laughed. "If that happens," he said, "I'll remember you told
me so." He stood up. "Let's see if Cheryl's through."

"What's she got?"

"A simple battery. Woman got jumped on by her ex-husband."

"Oh. What makes people want to act like that?"

"Your guess is as good as mine." Hall opened the office door and
looked out. "Yeah, she's got it wrapped up." They emerged from the
office and Sergeant Hall asked, "Cheryl, do you mind working with the
postal inspector for a while?"

"Which postal inspector now?" Cheryl asked resignedly, still looking at her report. Then she jumped to her feet. "Allen! I didn't see you
come in!"

"I know you didn't. The doctor says I can start working half time
now and move up to full time as I feel like it."

"That's terrific!" she said. "What are we working on?"

He produced a very theatrical sigh. "What have we been working on
forever and ever and ever?"

"Okay," she said, "let's get back on it."

On the way to his office he said, "It's got to be somebody easily
mobile—I remember one time saying something about it maybe being a
truck driver or a bush pilot. I don't really buy the truck driver, but are
there any bush pilots around?"

"Just Terry."

"Terry?"

"Holly's father. I know I told you—" She stopped. "No I didn't, I
told McCain. Anyhow, Terry's a charter pilot."

"Lady, if you can't tell the difference between me and McCain, you
need your eyes checked. So Terry's a pilot."

"Allen, I just don't think it could be him."

"Why? After the way he attacked Holly, I'd think—"

"He was drunk then," Cheryl interrupted. "Whoever killed Darling
Corey didn't do it drunk and on impulse. He thought it out."

"He ever have any connections to the post office?" asked Allen,
still unconvinced.

"Not that I know of," Cheryl said. "Well, I take that back. One year right at Christmas time they had some sort of flu epidemic in the post office and they hired a lot of high school boys as mail sorters—I know Terry, and Waymon Thomas, and Lee Gooch, and—oh, a lot of boys. But it was just a few weeks, and that was years ago."

"Where does he live?"

"East side of town. He still owns his family's farm now that his parents are dead, but I don't think he ever stays there. Allen, I just don't think his mind works that way. He's a creep, but he's not a sneaky creep."

"Well, let's keep him in mind, anyway."

They went in through the front of the post office, down the little hall past the mail sorting area, and into Allen's office. The secretary was gone. Allen began spreading papers on her rather bare desk. "First, let's make some sort of chart of what we do know," he said, "and work from that."

"McCain already did that."

"We do it again."

Two hours later they'd agreed that their man probably lived in Caddo County but had logical reasons to travel and to stay gone for lengthy periods of time. They didn't know whether he was black or white, but if he was white he had some sort of ties in the black community. They knew he had access to a print shop. They surmised he might at some time have had some (probably unpleasant) connection with the post office. But the biggest problem was the Polaroid identification machine. How could he—whether he was Terry Rhoads or anybody else—have known it was there?

"I knew it was there," Cheryl pointed out.

"How?"

"Because one time they were having a hearing about police pay raises, and the police decided to pack the council chamber. For some reason the closet was open then."

"Try to remember why."

She thought about it. "Oh! It was because they had some sound equipment stored there and they needed it."

"How many police were there?"

"I guess about thirty."

"But that's no use. None of them would have had any reason to be in Arkansas or Louisiana."

"All the commissioners could have known it was there," Cheryl pointed out. "And all the clean-up staff. And the press." She stopped. "Allen—"

But Allen had reached the thought the same time she had. "The press," he said. "They'd have access to presses to print the fake ID, and as for the whores—reporters use snitches as much as we do. Some of them could have found reasons to be in Arkansas and Louisiana as easy as a pilot could. But I wonder which ones *were* there?"

"Waymon might know," she said. "But I don't really know how to get hold of him; he's not employed by any newspaper. He's sort of a free-lancer; he calls himself a stringer." She picked up the phone and dialed. "Mama?" she said. "I need to talk to Waymon. Would you ask Charlotte how I can get hold of him?"

A moment later she said, "Then if it's all right with you, I'll come out there at six o'clock and talk to him and pick up Holly at the same time. Thanks—what? That's up to Holly if she wants to see him. But not while I'm there."

"He'll be there at six?" Allen asked.

"Yeah."

"What was that you were saying was up to Holly?"

"Terry. He wants to go out there this afternoon and see Holly and take her a doll."

"Sounds like *just* who Holly needs to see," Allen said.

"Yeah," Cheryl answered ruefully. "But I don't think she'll want to see him, and he won't dare try to get crossways of my mother. What do you want to do now?"

"It's almost one," Allen said. "Let's go get some lunch."

Halfway to the car, Cheryl stopped. "Allen?" she asked. "You know it could be Waymon? He's lived in Caddo County all his life. And he's got a family farm way out in the country besides his apartment, just like Terry does, so he could have hidden Darling Corey easily enough. And some of those papers he writes for are in Louisiana and Arkansas, and he travels a lot for them."

"Do you really think it is him?"

"Waymon? No, not really." She laughed. "He's too—insignificant."

"After lunch I'll go home and rest all afternoon. Not that I want to, but Jack told me to be sure not to get too tired. I'll meet you at your mother's house at six. But Cheryl. Just in case, let's go armed.''

Allen wasn't there yet. She went on in and sat down on the edge of the piano bench. With her jacket on to hide the shoulder holster, she didn't see how she was going to get a sweater on too, but she was considering trying. As usual in her mother's house, she was instantly freezing. "You want this chair?" Waymon asked from the depths of a platform rocker she'd always particularly disliked.

"Oh, no, thank you," she said. "Waymon, tell me something about all these reporters we've had in town lately."

"I can tell you they haven't made it easy for me," Waymon said, "because usually besides free-lancing I'm a stringer for five papers, and when they've got their own people in here they sure as hell don't need me."

"That does sound like a problem," Cheryl said. "How much have you gotten together with them, told stories, that kind of thing?"

"Some, of course, but not as much as I'd have liked. You know, I've always wanted to be on one of those really big papers. Oh well, one of these days—"

"Sure, one of these days," Cheryl agreed. "Give yourself time; it's early days yet." But she'd read some of Waymon's by-lined stories, and she doubted he'd ever make it, even if he wasn't the killer. And she didn't really think he was. She began to explain. "What I really wanted to know—" She turned more to face him; she barely noticed Charlotte coming in from the hall, preceded by an excitedly prancing Holly.

But Charlotte was not content to go unnoticed. "Look, Cheryl!" she said. "See what Waymon got me?"

"Uh-huh," Cheryl said. "Let me talk to Waymon for a minute."

"Cheryl, you're not looking," Charlotte said. "Look at it! I wasn't supposed to have it till my birthday, but I found it in his truck and then he had to go on and let me have it. Look, Cheryl! See, it's got my initials on it, 'DC' for Deborah Charlotte."

"Look, Mama," Holly urged.

Cheryl looked, then, and felt almost as if she'd been physically struck. She knew that bracelet, had several times inventoried it into property after making arrests. "Yes," she said slowly, "I see it. Did Waymon say where he got it?"

"No—Cheryl, what's wrong? Cheryl, what is it?"

But Waymon already knew what was wrong, and as Cheryl saw his face and reached for her pistol, encumbered as she was by the jacket, Waymon reached for Charlotte. Pulling her in front of him, he said, "Don't go for it, lady, I've got your sister." Cheryl heard a whir she couldn't identify as Waymon added, "I knew that would be a mistake. Damn it, why did she have to—"

"Knew what would be a mistake?" Cheryl interrupted. "Murdering Darling Corey, or giving her bracelet to my sister?"

Charlotte screamed. "He did what? Make him let me go! Cheryl, make him—"

"Hush, Charlotte," Cheryl said very quietly. "Be still. He won't hurt you."

"You think I can't?" His hand came from behind Charlotte. The whir Cheryl hadn't recognized had been the opening of a switchblade, and he put it against Charlotte's side. Charlotte screamed again. "You better not bet I can't. I meant to keep Charlotte," he said. "I meant to marry her after I got enough money. She's my clean little cousin; I've kept an eye on her. But I didn't give her that damn bracelet; she found it in the damn glove box. I'll kill her, yes I will, and I'll find another clean girl to marry, one that's not so nosy. Everybody always shoves me around—thinks I'm nothing—nobody can shove me around now. I'm the Man."

"It's no good, Waymon," Cheryl said, surprised that her voice remained steady. "We know, now, all of us. You can't kill us all. If you give up now, you won't get hurt. Let me have the knife, Waymon."

He jabbed the point of it into Charlotte's side; a trickle of blood began. Charlotte screamed a third time and, abruptly, went into what Cheryl recognized, quite academically, as a grand mal epileptic seizure. She's never done that before, Cheryl thought, or at least if she did I didn't know it, but the doctor always said she was epileptic; he said those outbursts of hers were a form of epilepsy—psychomotor, he said—she's never done this before.

Behind Cheryl, Holly screamed and ran out the front door. Waymon dropped Charlotte, and her mother, ignoring Waymon and his knife, knelt on the floor, sliding a cushion under Charlotte's head and catching hold, trying to keep her head from slamming against the floor. Waymon stood, apparently undecided, looking at the door Holly had left open, looking at Cheryl. Then he threw the knife; it missed Cheryl by an inch and stood quivering in the wood of the piano. He ran for the back door. "Don't follow me!" he shouted. "Nobody shoves me around any more. I've got a gun! I *will* kill you all—"

"Not now he doesn't have a gun," Cheryl said, "but he's going for one." She pulled hers from its holster. "Call the police, Mama!"

"Cheryl, you stay right here and let the police—"

"I can't, Mama, I *am* the police." And she was gone, out the back door right behind him.

He wasn't running for his truck as she expected. He was running around the side of the house. Here, Cheryl thought, he hid the gun here, this is where—she had a kaleidoscopic glimpse of the back yard, the gnarled grey clothesline poles, the multicolored bloom of the flower beds—Holly, Holly crying hysterically and climbing up the tailgate of Waymon's pickup truck. Poor Holly, she thought; she shouldn't see this, but I can't stop now—

He was headed for the rose trellis, and Cheryl caught a glimpse of a green metal cash box, half hidden behind the roses. "Stop or I'll shoot!" she shouted.

"You ain't got the guts!" he shouted back and dived for the cash box. But she didn't want to shoot him in the back, and she hesitated; he had the box open and his hand in it by the time she actually fired.

She walked over, then, and touched his temple, to check for a pulse. There wasn't a pulse. She didn't expect there to be a pulse.

Only then did she look in the metal box. He already had it in his hand, the revolver, the .32 Omega. She didn't touch it. It was part of a crime scene. You don't disturb crime scenes. Waymon wasn't there anymore, just the body that was one of the props, part of what it takes to be a crime scene.

Holly wasn't crying now.

Cheryl walked toward Waymon's pickup truck, to see why Holly wasn't crying now.

Holly wasn't crying now because Allen was holding her, holding her head to his shoulder. He looked over her to Cheryl. "She didn't see it, Cheryl," he said. "I saw what was coming. I was holding her. She didn't see it." He swallowed. "Guess I was about five minutes late."

"Or else I was early," she answered.

His gun was still in his holster. He hadn't drawn it at all. He couldn't because Cheryl was so far ahead of him and he couldn't run, not yet.

"Thank you, Allen," Cheryl said. "Are you all better now, Holly?"

"What happened to Aunt Charlotte?" Holly asked fearfully. "Is Waymon bad like my daddy? I didn't let my daddy come see me, but Waymon came to see Aunt Charlotte."

"Waymon was lots more bad than your daddy, but he can't hurt anybody anymore. And Aunt Charlotte was so scared she got sick. Can you run in the house now and see if she's better?"

"Uh-huh. Allen, I need down now."

Allen put Holly down, and Cheryl went to him. She felt his arms tight around her, strong and gentle, and she put her face against his shoulder, blindly, just the way Holly had. She wasn't sorry she had killed Waymon. Waymon hurt people and he shot Allen; it was Waymon's fault Allen had to suffer so much. And Waymon had killed a man she'd never met, that Jim McCain mourned. And Waymon had killed Darling Corey, and Darling Corey would never come back anymore, dancing on her light feet and throwing sparkle from her silver bracelet. And Waymon had killed Lucille Brantley and even Lucille's dirty, whiny, little two-year-old, who certainly didn't deserve to die. But now Waymon couldn't hurt anybody else because Waymon was gone.

But this corpse wore Waymon's face, and Waymon's face had laughed, and frowned, and talked, and eaten at the same table as Cheryl, and kissed Charlotte. And hurt Charlotte.

But nobody could hurt Cheryl now because she wasn't the frightened little girl she'd been when she was Holly's age; she was strong; she could protect herself. And if she was strong, if she could protect herself, why, then it was all right for her to love because nobody could hurt her when she was off guard. And she didn't have to be on guard around Allen because Allen wouldn't hurt her.

She didn't think any of it consciously, she just lifted her face to be kissed, and Allen, after a moment, seemed to realize why she had lifted her face and touched her lips with his. His lips were so warm she knew hers must feel cold, and she wondered why she was cold outside at the end of June. Allen tried to turn his head and hers followed, to stay with the warmth, and then his lips parted and Cheryl forgot everything else in the world except Allen's arms and Allen's mouth and Allen's body pressing against hers.

Only then the sirens stopped with a final raucous whine, and Cheryl, with a moan of protest, hid her face against Allen's chest.

"Your sergeant's here," he said to her.

"Tell him to go away?"

Allen, with a hint of laughter in his voice, "I don't think I can do that."

"I didn't really think so either," Cheryl said, and very reluctantly disentangled herself, keeping hold of one of Allen's hands. "Hi," she said to Sergeant Hall.

"Hi, yourself," the sergeant answered. "You're kind of making a habit of shooting people, aren't you?"

"No. Just two. That's not a habit."

"Cheryl, this one may get you in trouble. You shot him in the back. You know that, don't you?"

"Yes, and I didn't want to. But if you'll go look, you'll see why I had to."

The sergeant went and looked. He saw Waymon's body, still with one knee under him as he had been kneeling in the grass, preparing to turn, ready to kill Cheryl as he had killed so many others. He saw Waymon's right hand, and he saw in it the revolver that had been in the metal box. The revolver was a .32 Omega, and the way it was lying, he could read its serial number.

This was the .32 Omega that had been stolen from John Arnold almost two years before. This was the .32 Omega that killed a man in Bossier City and sent Allen Conyers to the hospital.

Still crouched beside the body, Hall asked, "How did you find out?"

"Allen and I were thinking it might be a reporter," Cheryl said, "because a reporter would have logical reasons to go to all the different places we knew this person had been and of course he'd have no trouble getting to a print shop. So we were going to talk with reporters, and we decided to start with Waymon just because he was— convenient. We'd even talked about it maybe being him, but I didn't think it was. But while I was talking to him my sister came in, wearing Darling Corey's bracelet. He tried to get to his gun. He'd stored it out here where anybody could find it. Why," she said, suddenly realizing, "Holly could have gotten hold of it; the box wasn't even locked or anything."

"Very unsafe practice to leave guns where children might get hold of them," Allen drawled. "I think that was the farthest thing from his mind. And Cheryl, he was looking at this rose trellis when I was telling you I was going to the post office that night, remember? Let me look at that thing." He looked at it. He wasn't laughing now; his mouth was set in a grim line, and Cheryl realized he must be mentally reviewing what the little revolver had cost him. When he reached out to touch the barrel of it his hand was shaking.

But then he backed away. "Holly'll be out in a minute," he said. "We don't want her coming over here."

They walked away from the body just as the kitchen door slammed and Holly came racing out and around the corner of the house. "Mama! Allen!" she shouted. "Listen! Aunt Charlotte's all better but some men came in a sort of white truck and they had this funny bed that folded up and down and had wheels on it, and they put Aunt Charlotte on it and they said they were going to take her to the hospital, and Granny said she had to go too. So," she added, suddenly puzzled, "if you have to go back to work and tell them about Waymon being very bad, who's going to stay with me? Because the nursery can't because it's at night and the nursery is just open at daytime. You won't leave me alone like my daddy did, will you?"

"Of course not," Cheryl said.

"But who's going to watch me then?"

"Will I do?" Allen asked. "Your mama and I both have to go to the police station, but we can take turns staying with you there till we get through. And you can draw pictures."

"Okay," Holly said. "Mama?"

"Hmm?" Cheryl was watching Lloyd, who was now taking photographs of the body and the revolver.

"Can I get a Popsicle?"

"Not right now, baby."

"Then can we go get a hamburger?"

"Not right now, baby." Lloyd had turned to say something to the coroner, who nodded. Apparently they'd decided the body could now be moved.

"Mama, I have a *good* idea! Since my daddy was bad like Waymon, and Mr. Judge Dors says he isn't my daddy anymore, can I have a new daddy? Mama, can Allen be my daddy?"

"Not right now, baby," Cheryl said mechanically, and then turned, suddenly aware of what Holly had said.

Allen was grinning, his eyes alight with mischief. "I was holding my breath to see if you were going to say that again," he confessed. "Holly, it takes longer to get a new daddy than to get a Popsicle and a hamburger. I think we can manage the Popsicle and the hamburger later today."

"How long does it take to get a daddy?" Holly asked impatiently.

"I don't know, honey." Allen was sitting on the ground now, talking with Holly. He carefully did not look at Cheryl, and she wondered whether it was because he was afraid of what she might see in his eyes. Lifting Holly, he stood up and repeated, "I don't know."

Cheryl wondered why she had ever been afraid of Allen. She no longer felt any need at all to punish him, or herself, for crimes other people had committed. As she took an impulsive step toward them, Holly said, "Maybe we could ask Mr. Judge Dors. He might know."

"I don't think that's necessary," Cheryl said, putting one arm around Allen and the other around Holly. "Maybe—maybe Allen could start being your daddy Friday."

"And then could he come live with us? Some of the kids have daddies that live with them."

"Uh-huh," Cheryl said. "And maybe—just maybe—sometime next year maybe we could get you a baby brother or sister. Would you like that?"

"Oh, boy!" Holly shouted. She started wriggling and Allen put her down, and she rushed across the yard yelling, "Sergean' Hall! Allen is gonna be my daddy and we're gonna get a baby!"

Allen turned toward Cheryl, his eyes glowing. Then his expression changed. "I'm in another damn ant hill!" he shouted. "Cheryl, if you laugh, so help me—"

But he began to laugh himself as Cheryl helped him get the ants off, and Sergeant Hall started toward them with a very astonished expression on his face.